BIG BAD BEAST

INTERSTELLAR BRIDES® PROGRAM: THE BEASTS - 4

GRACE GOODWIN

GET A FREE BOOK!

JOIN MY MAILING LIST TO BE THE FIRST TO
KNOW OF NEW RELEASES, FREE BOOKS,
SPECIAL PRICES AND OTHER AUTHOR
GIVEAWAYS.

http://freescifiromance.com

FIND YOUR INTERSTELLAR MATCH!

YOUR mate is out there. Take the test today and discover your perfect match. Are you ready for a sexy alien mate (or two)?

VOLUNTEER NOW!
interstellarbridesprogram.com

arlord Maxus, Underground Fight Club, Florida, Planet Earth

Human blood coated the floor of the fighting cage, sticky beneath my bare feet. Two human males faced me, watching. Waiting. I recognized fear, and these two reeked of it.

Guess they weren't as stupid as they appeared.

"Go, Rico. Fucking hit him."

The male issuing the order was called Python John. He stood to the side, behind his friend, Rico. Rico's broken nose leaked twin red trails of blood onto his lips, where he licked each drop away, grinning as if he enjoyed the taste. "Like blood? Eh, Wolf?"

Wolf. That was the name Snook, the fight club's owner, had given me after seeing my strangely striped hair. My black and silver streaks were compliments of the

Hive Integration Units and Nexus Six. The torture. Pain. Experiments. Years of experiments.

Now that I was free, only two things mattered to me. One, finding my mate, and two, eliminating the never-ending stream of Hive Trackers who hunted me. The Hive were relentless. Nexus Six wanted me back under his control. His monster. His killer.

I'd rather be dead.

I didn't care what the humans called me. Snook paid me to fight and didn't ask questions. I didn't want any of these humans asking questions. I wasn't supposed to be here, on Earth. I was an alien, an Atlan warlord and contaminated Hive Soldier, presumed dead. For now that was exactly the way I wanted it.

"Go ahead. Hit me." I taunted the humans, knew they were exhausted whereas I was bored, my beast irritated by the distraction from the only thing that mattered—finding *her*. Our mate.

"Shut up, dog boy." Python John liked to run his mouth more than he wanted to use his fists.

I smiled at him, which made him grit his teeth and glare. Still, he did not attack.

Python John circled to stand shoulder to shoulder with Rico, both males staring at me, working up their courage.

"You first," Rico ordered. "You go in and I'll follow."

"Get on with it." I held my arms out to my sides, exposing my bare chest and ribs. My fighting shorts clung, snug against my ass and thighs.

Rico held his fists in front of his face and swung his leg out wide, in an arcing kick. I swatted him away, annoyed, and stepped forward. "Fight, you cowards. I don't have all fucking day."

Rico snarled at me and spit on the mat that covered the floor of the fighting cage, his blood bright red. "Fuck you, you big motherfucker."

Oh yes, I'd been around these humans long enough to participate in what they called *talking trash.* "If I'd fucked your mother, you wouldn't be so small and weak."

The two males moved to surround me, one on each side. I could pound them into dust within minutes, but that did not please the spectators. Snook wanted his customers happy and drunk and spending money on alcohol, drugs, and placing bets.

As if my thoughts of him had manifested him in the flesh, Snook appeared, walking toward the edge of the cage. He spoke to all three of us.

"Take your time, gentlemen. The betting is just getting started." Snook looked up at me, catching my eye, and tapped his cheek, a symbol that he wanted me to allow one or both of these fools to strike me a few times. He paid extra for each hit I allowed the humans to land. Annoying, but every human dollar helped me expand my search for my mate. Small price to pay.

I dipped my chin so Snook would know I understood. He grinned and wandered away.

My beast growled, the sound escaping my throat before I could contain it. We wanted to kill that human. Protect the females of this planet. Males like him should be dead already.

Fucking humans. No clue what was important, sacred.

"Come on, wolf man," Rico goaded me, and I

returned my attention to the two men waiting for me to injure them. I took a slow, deep breath and processed a thousand different scents...and froze.

My beast roared inside my skull, fighting for freedom. Insane. Enraged.

That scent, the barest hint of a *female*.

MATE.

I fell to my knees, the beast so strong that I wrapped my arms around my head and prayed to the gods, to all gods, that my beast would retreat. Revealing myself to these humans would be a disaster. They would hunt me. Call their authorities. Those idiots would do the only thing they could to protect their people. They would call the Interstellar Brides Processing Center and send the Atlan guards and Prillon warriors there to retrieve me. My mating fever would rage. I'd be transported to Atlan and executed within hours.

NO! Mate!

I held the images in my mind. Atlan prison. Human police. The beast grumbled but retreated, the Hive integrations once more communicating with the more primitive side of me, keeping me sane far longer than any other warlord with Mating Fever that I'd ever heard of.

"What the fuck?" Python John walked around me and launched a kick at my head. His foot connected with my temple. My head jerked to the side. Jumping back, he bounced on the balls of his feet and struck again. His second kick landed on my jaw. My beast growled. If I didn't stop this asshole, my beast would.

Focus.

Impossible. *She* was real. I had found her. My mate.

Someone in this shithole of a fight club, among this

scum of humanity, carried my mate's scent on him. His clothes? His *skin?*

I groaned and allowed the muscles in my shoulders to twitch. The crowd was screaming, losing their minds now that I appeared to be at a loss. Python John kicked me in the back. I did not move.

Not wishing to take a third blow to the head, I stood and focused on my opponents even as I analyzed my situation. I had not considered that my mate, once I found her, would already belong to another. My beast raged at the thought, fighting to break free. I pounded on my chest like an animal, taunted the two humans in the cage across from me.

Python John and Rico watched me, concern in their eyes. Two kicks to the head, and yet, I ignored them. They were beneath my notice, especially now.

She was close, nearby but not *here*. Her scent was a whisper to my enhanced senses, barely there. Not *inside the fight club*. Where was she? Where the fuck was she?

I pulled air into my lungs, searching for the smallest trace of her.

There! Faint, so faint. Flowers and honey and...blood? Metal?

What the fuck?

The strange combination went straight to my cock. My body hardened at the thought of her, even as I nearly convinced myself it was all in my head. A dream. Wishful thinking. Perhaps I was finally losing my mind.

MATE! My beast insisted. He sensed her as well. And she was close. So fucking close.

"Wolf! Wolf! Wolf!" A handful of young, overeager males stood near the cage and began the chant. The crowd took up their cry until at least a hundred human males were chanting the name of the animal Snook had insisted I take as my symbol.

"Wolf! Wolf! Wolf!"

Perhaps my female would be close enough to hear their chant, to wonder at the prowess of the male who inspired such fervor. Perhaps she listened now, her pussy growing wet and eager. Her nipples peaked. Her breasts ripe and round and so sensitive I could make her come by sucking their hard tips into my mouth.

"Wolf! Wolf! Wolf!"

Every person in the area seemed to be cursing or encouraging one or all three of us fighters. They cursed one another, the spectators shouting commands with excitement and rage in equal measure.

I watched them all. I waited. I looked at every face in the area, scanned the voices I could hear with my Hive implants. Filtered the noise with senses both Atlan and Hive.

She was not here. Not in this fight club, not with these humans. The knowledge was both agony and relief.

My beast was getting stronger. More insistent. Even with the added control the Hive implants afforded, I was running out of time. I couldn't afford to blow this fight, not if I wanted to stay on Earth. But my beast would not wait much longer to hunt our female.

"Come on!" I bellowed the word at my two opponents, hoping to goad them into action so I could end this. I cracked my knuckles and grinned at the two humans.

Both males launched at once. I allowed their strikes, a handful, as the crowd became insane, screaming for more blood. I counted ten strikes. Two small cuts began to bleed on my cheek. That would mean an extra month's rent, less fighting, more private time with my female.

"Is that it?" I asked, once the flurry of eager punching had ceased.

"Fuck. You!" Rico's nose still bled. If I had to guess, I would say the last elbow I threw had cracked his cheekbone. Added insult to injury. I was toying with them, and they fucking knew it.

Python John leaped onto my back. "You are a big fucker. You asshole. Now what you gonna do, huh?" The male wrapped his arms around my neck in an attempt to close off my airway. His legs wrapped around my waist, ankles locked.

Rico charged me. I moved at full speed, punching him in the nose just hard enough to send him stumbling backward.

The crowd screamed with bloodlust and I obliged. Reaching behind me, I lifted Python John up over my head like he weighed no more than a small child, and threw him down on the mat, his back hitting with a loud *thud*.

Both males climbed to their feet, and I had to give them credit for persistence if not intelligence.

They charged. I pummeled both with my fists. Not too hard, I was careful not to kill them. Blood flew through the air; the cage became soaked with the scent. Human skin was so fragile, so very easy to tear.

"Fuck." Python John spit blood from his mouth to land on the mat near the metal fencing. A piece of his tooth went with it. "Snook don't pay me enough for this shit."

John was large for a human. As was Rico. Both well

over average for a male from this planet, which meant the tops of their heads nearly reached my chin. Well-muscled. Street fighters. Cruel.

There were no rules in the cage. Anything was allowed short of killing a man.

I'd done enough killing to last several lifetimes.

Rico paced to one side of the cage, moving to my left as he spoke to Python John. "If you'd stop snorting all your money up your nose, you wouldn't have to fight."

"Fuck you, Rico." Python John moved opposite Rico, coming around me on my right. He wiped the blood dripping into his right eye away with the back of his wrist.

"You know what to do." Rico glanced at Python John for confirmation. When his partner dipped his chin in agreement, I almost shouted encouragement. Finally. I could end this and track down that scent. Find her. My mate. The human female who could save me.

Grinning now, eager, I waited for them to make their move.

Both males walked *away* from me toward the edge of the cage.

What the fuck?

Two of Snook's lackeys were waiting to slide long, wicked-looking daggers through the cage's openings. Both men wrapped their hands around the blade hilts and turned to face me.

Seemed Snook intended to force my hand, give me no choice but to kill.

The crowd's roar increased in volume as my two opponents lifted the daggers and showed them to the gathered humans. Frantic to place their wagers, the humans outside the cage scurried like starving rats to give money to those who registered their bets.

"Put the blades down. I do not wish to kill you." I had to warn them. I was an Atlan warlord who fought with honor. If they persisted on this course of action, they would die.

"You're the one who's going to do the dying, pretty wolf man." Python John had a huge smile on his face, his front tooth ragged and uneven. I assumed the other half of that tooth was already on the cage floor.

I held up both hands, palms facing out in the universal sign of appeal. "Do not force me to kill you. Please. Put down the weapons."

"Enough of this bullshit," Rico muttered. He and John paced the edge of the cage, stalling. My suspicions were confirmed when I spotted Snook seated at an elevated table near the exit. He caught Rico's gaze and dipped his chin, giving the two males fighting me the signal to continue.

I did not bother to shout over the din of the roaring humans, all so very eager to see blood spilled. I held Rico's gaze. He did not smile as Python John did, but there was death in Rico's eyes. A love of killing. A clawing need for power. I had seen the look before. Too many times. Too many fights. Of the two, Rico was more dangerous, and I would not make the mistake of turning my back on him.

I held Rico's gaze. "Get on with it. I tire of this game."

"This ain't no fucking game," Rico shouted as he shifted the blade from hand to hand.

"We're going to kill you, motherfucker!" Python John was red-faced, eyes glazed with excitement. And fear.

"Put them down. You will not collect payment from Snook if you are dead."

With synchronized shouts, Rico and Python John rushed me from both sides. They each attempted to capture one of my wrists with their free hand and stab my exposed side with the other.

I moved with blurring speed, utilizing the Hive implants that pulsed with power just beneath my skin. I was not human, nor was I Atlan. I was more. And less. I was contaminated. A beast.

A predator with a barely controlled monster inside me. My beast recognized the threat and demanded to taste their blood. He pushed at the edges of my control, his rage complete. Total. Consuming.

Fuck.

They slashed at my sides, each one scoring a thin slice through skin where they'd hoped to stab deep.

The crowd screamed with excitement as my blood dripped to the floor of the cage for the first time. Red, just like a human's. The sight appeared to cause mayhem. Chaos. A frenzy.

Animals. Humans were animals.

The cuts were shallow, mere annoyances. I would not bleed to death, but I would require the use of a ReGen wand after this fight. I'd paid well to have one of the Atlan guards at the Interstellar Brides Processing Center smuggle the device to me, along with a pair of mating cuffs. I would not have opportunity to use either if I lost focus and allowed these two fools to kill me.

Rico and Python John regrouped on the opposite side of the cage as the rest of the humans screamed for more. More blood. More pain. More. More. More.

"Put the blades down and you have my word I will not kill you."

"Fuck you, Wolf. You aren't in any position to make deals," Python John snarled.

I sighed. Python John had no idea exactly how wrong he was.

The two men rushed me again. With a roar, I moved like lightning to wrap a hand around each of my opponents' necks. Grip harsh, I squeezed until both men's faces turned red, then purple. They swung their limbs wildly, trying to reach me with fists and feet.

They looked ridiculous, like children swinging at a statue.

The crowd went eerily silent, waiting to see what I would do.

The quiet didn't last long as one loud voice yelled from somewhere in the crowd. "Kill them!"

Chaos erupted as every human in the club seemed to lose control of their emotions, their minds. They screamed and shoved like wild animals fighting over a carcass.

Disgusted, I lifted both men a bit higher, onto the tips of their toes and found Snook in his seat, watching. Waiting.

Bastard. Fucking, cock-sucking bastard.

When he met my gaze, he was smiling in triumph. I had refused to fight to the death. He had ensured I must. Fucking asshole. I was like a dog in the pit now. Nothing more than an animal to him. An investment. Fight or die.

Fury ripped through me. I was a warlord, a male of honor. I would not kill at the behest of this monstrous human. My beast, however, did not mind in the least. He was hungry for blood. For victory. For any kind of release. We had not seen true battle in months. Nor fucked a female.

Disgusted, I threw the two humans to the far side of the cage where they both rolled onto their hands and knees.

"Stay down!" I bellowed at the two fighters.

Light reflected off metal. I turned, prepared to face another attack of some kind. But the flash was not from a weapon, but from a naming badge an older male wore on his shirt as he walked the edge of the fighting cage. Watching us.

The other humans seemed to know who he was, for they moved back without instruction, making way for him to pass.

Who was he? And what the fuck was he doing?

Distracted, I focused my attention on him, read his name from the badge. *Wayne.* He wore a uniform, not for battle, more like what I had seen human firefighters wear. His hair was completely gray, his face lined. But his eyes were sharp. Assessing.

And he smelled like...*her.*

My beast exploded into my mind like a separate entity, pushing and clawing to reach the human male. Heat burned through my gaze and I closed my eyes, afraid they would glow and give me away. Reveal that I was not human.

The thud of two feet pounding on the cage's mat floor had me turning. I opened my eyes. Python John was charging me, knife held low.

I allowed him to get close. Closer.

With a bellow I hoped sounded human, I lifted him

over my head and tossed his body like a sack of grain, up and over the top of the cage.

He fell, his torso crashing into the few spectators too slow, or too drunk, to get out of the fucking way.

Wayne, the human I needed to follow, raised his brow, and looked up at me.

I stared back. He knew where she was. My mate.

With a sideways glance at Python John, who was staggering to his feet with the help of a few men, Wayne watched until Python John was upright then looked back to me. The elder human shook his head like a disapproving father and turned to walk away.

Fuck. I didn't have time for this shit.

Where was Rico?

As if on cue, Rico appeared before me. He tossed his knife between his palms. Was that supposed to intimidate me?

"End this," I ordered.

Rico didn't need further encouragement.

I threw him even farther than his friend.

The crowd was frantic. Screaming. Chanting my name.

I scanned for Wayne, found him just as he disappeared through the locked metal door that was a shortcut to the parking area.

Fuck.

I didn't wait for Snook's people to unlock the fighting cage. I climbed up and over, jumping to land on the ground next to where Python John had smashed into the spectators.

Wayne was getting away.

Mate!

My beast had a one track fucking mind, as did I.

I took three steps toward the door before Snook stood in my path.

"Get the fuck out of my way."

"You should have killed them."

Completely out of patience, I lifted the human by his shoulders and set him aside. My beast had even less patience than I and there was only one thing he cared about at the moment.

Mate. Mine.

 *ivian Davis*

I SAT in the back of the private ambulance Snook provided and dealt out the cards for yet another round of solitaire. As usual, he'd offered to let me sit next to him and watch the fights. I declined. Again. Politely. I sat in the rig. I waited. I patched up the fighters who needed stitches or fluids. Sometimes antibiotics. On the rare occasion, we would actually take them to a nearby hospital, where I would describe picking up the wounded man after a bar brawl or street fight.

In this neighborhood the doctors and nurses didn't even bat an eye. No one asked questions because no one wanted to know. Gunshot wounds were much more common in the emergency room on a Friday night. Someone who had a concussion, a few lacerations, or an internal bleed from a fistfight was generally low priority.

Judging by the screaming roar of the crowd coming from inside, tonight was going to be a hospital night.

With a sigh, I laid out my cards on top of the empty stretcher. I could play the game on my phone app, but I liked the tactile feeling of shuffling the deck, placing the cards. Counting them in my hands. Touching the phone screen lacked a certain satisfaction. I liked to feel things. Real things. Which meant I was old, or old-school. Maybe both.

"Jesus, Mary, and Joseph." Snook's driver, Wayne, cursed as he hopped up into the driver's seat. He'd gone inside to take a look around. He liked to assess the fighters, guess what kind of injuries we'd be dealing with.

"That bad?"

"That bad. They're like animals tonight. Screaming for blood." He and I both knew he wasn't talking about the fighters.

"Maybe it's just too much tequila." I tried to laugh, but his warning made me anxious. There was something different about tonight, something that had me on edge. Nervous. I had no logical reason, just gut instinct. But when I felt like this, I paid attention.

Wayne gave a non-committal grunt from the driver's seat of the ambulance.

I was working tonight because Snook paid well, in cash. I needed the money to pay for my girls' school. Besides, I'd done worse jobs for far less money. I had no intention of looking a gift horse in the mouth.

"Viv, it's bad tonight. You stay the hell out of there." Wayne's intense stare was focused on the large metal door that divided the two large sections of the old parking garage. Fights on one side, spectator parking and this ambulance on the other.

"No problem. I don't want to see it." I counted three cards and flipped the small collection face up. Damn. Nothing to play. "It's bad enough cleaning up the mess afterward."

Wayne lit a cigarette. He knew I hated the smoke, but we had all the doors open and he exhaled out the driver's side window, away from where I sat in the back.

"One of these days, one of them boys is going to end up dead."

"No."

"It's inevitable. You know that."

"Not while I'm here." But I knew he was right. The fights seemed to be growing more and more violent, as did the crowd Snook's club seemed to attract. "I don't do corpses."

"We'll see. Tonight may be our lucky night."

"Shut-up, Wayne." I'd been thinking the exact same thing the last few weeks. What would I do when the first dead body was carried out that door?

My paramedic's uniform pants were suddenly too tight, my belt digging into my stomach until I fought down vomit. The button-up shirt's starched collar circled my neck like a noose. I wouldn't do dead. No matter how much Snook offered to pay me. Stitching up a cut was one thing. Carting corpses was completely different. No. *Hell no.*

I gathered up the cards and tossed them aside, no longer interested in the game.

Wayne took a deep drag on his cigarette, watching me the entire time with those wise, old eyes.

I'd been born in this shithole. I'd survived this long. I knew everyone and everyone knew me. If Snook really did start allowing the boys to fight to the death—

The central door to the parking garage slammed open, the heavy metal banging on the concrete wall. A bare-chested giant walked toward me. He had to be close to seven feet tall. Maybe taller. His lips were full, jaw cut like a marble statue. And his eyes. Whoa, his eyes. They were so pale a blue they looked like they were glowing at me out of the shadows.

He bled from multiple cuts on his body—his magnificent, muscular, holy-mother-of-God body. Normally I could look and dismiss a man's physique. Not right now. So much for professional detachment.

God! I could not stop staring. More like drooling.

As he came closer, I froze in place, hypnotized. Couldn't even blink. Damn. He was the sexiest thing I'd ever seen. Ever. Not only was he professional-basketball-player tall, he completed the look with broad shoulders and powerful thighs. His chest was thicker than any man's had a right to be, and his torso tapered into a perfect V shape filling his fighter's shorts. His thick hair shone in the artificial light. The black and silver strands were unique. Striking. More than long enough to bury my fingers in and tug his mouth where I wanted him to go. Lips. Neck. Nipples...

Lower. I wanted his mouth on my pussy, his hands holding my thighs open as he—

Shit. I knew I was blushing now, but the sun had set, leaving the yellowish tinge of recessed lights to illuminate the covered parking area. Yellow would hide my blush very well. Thank God.

I should look away, stop gawking. He moved like he was aware of every cell in his body. Where it was. What it was doing. He was pure, raw power, coiled to strike. No shoes either. He wore nothing but a pair of plain black shorts that did absolutely nothing to hide the rather giant bulge between his legs. It drew my gaze like a beacon, and a shiver raced over my skin. He could feast on my pussy, and then I could ride that big cock for dessert.

God. He was hot. Sex-on-a-stick hot.

A very tall stick.

I blinked, hard, and looked away before he caught me and I embarrassed myself even more. But damn. Just damn. My nipples had hardened to eager peaks. My panties had to be soaked. Every bit of skin felt sensitive, primed for his touch. And I felt ridiculous. Sure, he was handsome. Sensual. I wanted to jump on him, wrap my legs around him, and never, ever let go. But I couldn't. Wouldn't. I was a professional and he was bleeding. Injured.

I was an experienced woman, not a hormonal teenager.

I had to get a grip on myself. Get. A. Grip.

The massive sex god was followed out the door by Snook himself. The two appeared to be arguing.

"I'm done." The giant's voice rumbled like an echo from a bass drum. So deep. Rich. I swallowed hard and tried to pay attention to the conversation as every feminine part of my body responded to that voice. I wanted him talking dirty to me as he pounded into me with that massive—

"I own you, Wolf. You'll be here next Friday, or I'll send the boys to bring you in."

The giant shrugged as if he truly didn't give a shit about Snook or his threats. Wolf—that had to be his fighting name—didn't even look at Snook. His gaze was searching the parking garage, darting everywhere, until his gaze locked onto me.

"Shit." Wayne cursed.

I stared back. Couldn't look away. Didn't want to.

I wanted him. Inside me. On top of me. Under me.

Down, girl.

Enough. I didn't drool over bleeding patients who needed my help. And I didn't drool over men who were tangled up with Snook. Snook ran this part of town. He was a criminal, through and through. A bad guy who occasionally did good things for the community. He paid me, so I worked. And if it weren't Snook running the dark side of this neighborhood, it would be someone else, someone worse. There was always someone worse.

One of Wolf's cheeks was bruised, a small bit of dried blood clinging to his skin, but the slight discoloration did not detract from the godlike lines of his profile.

What the hell was happening to me? I had never, never ever reacted like this to any man. Insane. I'd lost my mind.

This was not good. Not good at all.

Snook cleared his throat to demand my attention. With an act of sheer will, I looked away from Wolf and waited for Snook to speak.

"Stitch him up and get him the fuck out of here."

I didn't respond, but my attention returned to Wolf. His glistening skin. His pale, perfect eyes.

Snook cursed. "Fuck. What a mess. Clean him up and make it quick. Wayne, when she's done with him, bring her inside." Snook looked from Wayne back to the giant, his scowl deepening. "You should have killed them."

"I'm done." The large man's voice dropped an octave, his anger evident in the slow rumble that moved through me, straight to my core. I licked my lips, trying to taste him on the air. Which was just dumb. So stupid. But everything about him made me feel a bit crazy and out of control.

I wondered what would he be like in bed? Would he go wild or would he be slow and gentle? Would he want to hold me afterward, or carry me to the shower and fuck me against the tile like a wild man as hot water poured down over us?

I was not a small woman. I was a bit taller than average and a lot curvier. I had an ass and round thighs and an abdomen that had carried twins. I was no thin little girl. But this guy was massive. Strong. He could hold me against the wall and have his wicked way with me.

Damn it. He was jaw-droppingly gorgeous. He was so far out of my league we weren't even on the same planet.

So why did I want to use the scissors I had in the medical kit to cut his shorts off his body and jump him? Ride that hard body until I passed out with exhaustion?

Bad, Vivian. Bad. I was too experienced and too smart to get tangled up with one of Snook's fighters.

"You made a mistake in there," Snook insisted. "A big, fucking mistake."

"I do not kill for sport." So formal. Wolf's words were clipped, his pronunciation perfect, as if he'd gone to private boarding school surrounded by rich snobs.

Snook ran his hand through his hair, clearly agitated. "I've seen it in your eyes. I know the look. You're a killer."

"I fought in the war. I served my time. I'm done with killing." He spoke to Snook, but he was looking at me. Did he want me to know this about him? Why?

Which war? So he was a soldier? That made him even hotter.

Snook's face was turning red with anger. I had never seen him like this before. Clearly he was not used to being challenged or, worse, defied in public. Something must have gone wrong with the fight. "You humiliated them. They'll want blood."

"They'll have to do better than those little knives you gave them." Wolf looked down his nose at Snook, reached out, and wrapped his hand around Snook's neck. Squeezed. "I told you I would not fight to the death. You tried to force my hand. You're lucky I don't kill you."

Knives? This fight club was all about boxing or mixed martial arts. There were no knives.

Snook's hands wrapped around the giant's wrist and pulled with no effect whatsoever. None. Jeez, this guy was even stronger than he looked.

"Fuck. Fine. You're finished."

"Apologize to me, as a man of honor, or I will be forced to end your life."

"Fuck y—"

The air that should have been behind the second word coming out of Snook's mouth was gone. Wolf snarled. His biceps flexed, and Snook dangled off the ground, feet swinging like a child's as Wolf held him there, no signs of strain on his face. None. He wasn't shaking. Hell, he hadn't even adjusted his stance.

Holy shit. Snook was not small. And this guy held him in the air with *one hand*?

My entire body shivered with lust. Raw. Visceral. This was more than attraction.

"This is insane." I was talking to myself, but my body was not listening. Bitch had a mind of her own, and she wanted to jump out of the ambulance and on top of a complete stranger. A dangerous, sexy, mysterious stranger big enough to scare the infamous Miami Snook. Which, in all the years I'd grown up running the streets in this neighborhood, had seemed impossible.

Snook gave up the fight, lifted his hands to the sides of his head, and tried to speak.

"Sorry, Wolf. Sorry. My bad." Each word was more rasp than spoken voice, but Wolf released him. Snook stepped back until he was beyond the larger man's reach, took a deep breath, and then turned his attention to me. "Stitch him up and get inside. Rico and John need your attention."

Both of them? I looked at Wolf again. Rico *and* John? He'd fought both of those brutes *at the same time?*

I looked more closely at Wolf's cuts. He was bleeding, but there were no pumping arteries or deep stab wounds. Nothing major. I would stitch him up, and he would live. I had no idea about the conditions of Rico or John. "How bad are they? Do I need to take care of them first?"

I'd taken care of both men in the past. Didn't care for either of them.

"They're downing shots at the bar. They can wait." Snook tossed a thick envelope I assumed held my weekly payment onto the stretcher next to me, then turned on his heel and walked away.

I scrambled down from the back of the ambulance

and moved out of the way so the sexy, bleeding fighter could step up and climb inside.

His hand brushed mine as he passed and I shivered, bunched my hand into a fist to keep myself from reaching for him.

Wolf's weight caused the rig to dip. He sat on the stretcher, his head nearly touching the ceiling, and lifted an arm to inspect his wounds on that side. By my count, there were at least four large gashes that would require stitching. Which meant I got to *touch*.

I climbed in to sit opposite him, looked from his torso to his face and forgot how to breathe. He was staring at me now, but his eyes didn't look human. Were they glowing silver?

Frozen like a deer in headlights, we stared at one another for long seconds. I swayed, suddenly light-headed.

"Breathe, female. I will not allow anyone to harm you." Even as he bossed me, Wolf looked at me like he wanted to eat me alive and spit out my bones. Truth be told, I wasn't opposed to the eat-me-alive part of the scenario as long as he started in the right place.

I was no young virgin. I was a grown-ass woman. A professional.

"I can take care of myself."

"No, you will not. Not anymore."

3

M axus

Take care of herself?

No. She. Was. Mine. The beast knew this fact the moment we'd caught her scent. Seeing her, hearing her voice, only confirmed what the beast already knew.

Mine!

I was acutely aware of her. The way she moved. The smell of the scented soap she must use on her skin. Her full lips and generous curves caused me to burn with the need to taste every inch of her. She was a female in her prime. Fully formed. Unafraid.

My cock reacted to her presence as if she'd wrapped her mouth around the hard length and sucked me deep. The painful throbbing between my legs pulled my attention from the lacerations in my sides. They were not significant. They would heal soon enough.

I was injured but not enough to curtail my need to take my mate and fuck her senseless. Put the mating cuffs on her wrists and make her scream my name as I pumped my seed into her body.

"Are you going to help me or stare at me all night?" I challenged her, hoping it would erase the wary look from her green and gold eyes. Hazel, humans called the color. With her dark red hair, I found her to be beyond beautiful. Soft. Perfect. She was fucking perfect, and she was mine. I had found her. Thank the gods. My mate.

"I'm a professional. I do not stare at my patients."

"What if I want you to look at me?"

"Shut up and hold your arm up out of my way so I can stitch you up." She climbed into the small vehicle and moved a stool into place so she could sit opposite me where I rested on an odd bed that sat atop a metal frame with wheels. The bed would be no good for fucking. I would have to take my new mate somewhere else. Somewhere safe.

Somewhere private so I could shove her against the wall and make her come. Bury my tongue deep in her pussy. Taste her wet heat. Claim her. Fuck her. Over. And over. And over...

"Do you want me to numb the cuts before I do this?" She wasn't even looking at me. Instead she worked quickly and efficiently, opening her packets and gadgets. She put on a pair of stretchy gloves, then smeared a dark brown liquid over the first wound. She paused and looked up at me. "Well?"

"No need." My Hive integrations were very effective at reducing pain. A warlord who did not feel the pain of his wounds in battle was a more efficient killer.

"I figured you'd say that." She sighed and leaned in close enough that her warm breath heated my skin. She held a small white device in her hand. "I'm going to use staples. Less infection. I'll try to make this quick. And I'll give you some antibiotics to take for a few days."

Her statements did not require a response. I waited for her touch. When her small fingers pressed on my flesh, working to close the wounds, I nearly groaned aloud. The short bite of what she called staples was nothing to the crackling awareness of her fingers on my skin.

The beast roared inside my head like a caged storm. I'd been struggling to control him from the moment those idiots had drawn their knives. My beast wanted more than blood. He demanded total and complete annihilation. Had I given the beast his way, Rico and Python John would have been torn in pieces and left on the floor of that cage.

As it was, I'd had to throw them over the fence and into the crowd to save their lives. They'd been injured, but they were alive.

The beast, however, was still enraged. Fighting to break free. Except now he had a new target. Her. A mate. His mate.

Years of training, of torture, of learning to battle my beast saved my female from being taken here. Now. The beast was out of control. I could not allow him to come out, not until she knew the truth and was already mine.

"What is your name?" I demanded.

She shook her head. "We don't do names around here, *Wolf*."

"My name is Maxus."

"Shhh." She glanced toward the front of the vehicle, and I noticed an older human male I had not seen before. He watched my interaction with the female with interest, almost as if he believed he was protecting her. "Don't. I don't want to know."

The male in the front of the vehicle lifted one hand to reveal a small human weapon called a handgun. The projectile it emitted would do little more than irritate me, but any attack now, with my mate unclaimed and vulnerable, would send my beast into an uncontrollable rage.

I met the male's gaze. "I would never harm a female."

"You try anything and I'll put one between your eyes."

Indeed. I wondered if the elderly male was capable of such precision. His gaze did not waver, and I suspected he was. Fuck. I was slipping. This female's presence combined with my irritation with the human known as Snook had caused me to lose focus. The human could have attacked me unaware. I could not allow that to happen again. Not now that I had a female to protect.

The fact that the older male appeared to be protecting my mate saved his life.

"Calm down. No one is shooting anyone. I'm almost done." She used her small gadget to sting me three more times before leaning back to inspect her work. "Okay. Put that arm down. I need to do the other side."

I obeyed her instructions and chose to ignore the elderly human male. My mate appeared to trust him, which meant she did not consider him a threat.

The scent of sweet fruit and citrus drifted to me from her hair. I wondered if the scent was perfume, shampoo, or just her. Her dark red hair was pulled back into one of the pony's tails—at least that was what I believed humans called it. The pony's tail left her long neck exposed. I longed to lean over and kiss her skin. Nip at her. Taste her. I would then kiss along the soft angle of her jaw until I reached those plump lips.

She glanced up at me through the corner of her eye. "I can feel you staring."

"You are beautiful beyond measure."

The elderly man snorted. "Laying it on thick, boy."

My mate's neck turned pink. As did her cheek.

Fascinating. Was she aroused? Embarrassed? I needed to know everything about her.

"I speak the truth." I stared down at my female. "You are beautiful."

"I think that fight rattled your brains around inside that head of yours."

"That fight was of little consequence. I am fully functional."

She froze, the stinging of her staples stopped as well. "You call this fully functional?"

I shrugged, happy to stare into her eyes. "I have suffered much worse. These wounds matter not."

"Jesus." She shook her head and returned to her task, mumbling to herself. "Doesn't matter. You're crazy, you know that? All you fighters are the same. So macho. Nothing hurts. Yeah, right." She placed the last staple with a bit of extra pressure, as if annoyed with me.

"Please, female, honor me with your name."

She ran her fingers over my ribs. Checked the staples. She poured a clear liquid over small, white squares and used the wet pieces to wipe the remaining blood from my sides. "Vivian. My name is Vivian."

"Thank you, Vivian." My mate's name was Vivian. "I

vow to honor your gift." Vivian. A unique name, as befitted this female.

She wiped her cold, wet, white square along my opposite side and shook her head. "You're an odd cat. You know that?"

"I am not a feline."

She chuckled. "Oh yeah, you're a wolf."

"I am Maxus."

"No last name? Just Maxus?"

"Where I am from, I do not require more than one name to be known."

"Not surprising." Her slight smile had me gripping the edge of the metal bed frame to refrain from reaching for her. Had she given me a compliment? Judged me a worthy male?

I could not afford to make any mistakes with her. My beast was too close to the surface. I hung on to my sanity by sheer force of will. My mating fever was nearly beyond my control. If she refused me, if she denied me—worse, if she *ran*—the beast would take over and I would be lost to his madness. His primitive urges. His instinctive need to hunt, to kill, to fuck.

I would hurt her and many others before they managed to kill me. With my enhanced Hive implants, I could destroy cities. Kill hundreds, perhaps thousands of humans.

That could not be allowed to happen. And now that I'd found my mate, it would not. I just needed to claim her. Put the mating cuffs around my wrists—and hers. Dedicate my life to protecting and caring for her. She was the only thing that mattered now.

Vivian finished with her wet squares and patted my skin dry with a cloth. I watched, fascinated, as she placed a shiny strip of white fabric on top of my first wound and secured it with tape. When she had covered all my wounds, she pulled the gloves from her hands and tossed them into a red basket with the rest of the bloody mess. "That ought to do it. I'll give you a staple remover. Wait at least a week to take them out." She opened a cabinet and lifted a small bottle from one of the shelves. She held out the bottle. When I didn't reach for it, she opened my hand, placed the bottle in my palm, and wrapped my fingers around the plastic. "Take these three times a day until they're gone."

"What are these?"

"Antibiotics. To prevent infection."

I placed my free hand over hers to hold her close. I wasn't ready to break contact. "There is no need." My Hive integrations would attack any bacteria or virus that entered my system. I did not require this type of medical assistance. A ReGen pod would be nice, but I would make do with the ReGen wand I had hidden at my dwelling. I'd allowed her to tend me for one simple reason...I needed her touch.

"Yes, there is. You were in that filthy cage fighting with two filthy men. Take them."

I couldn't tell her the truth. Not yet. She appeared to be concerned for my health rather than terrified by my size. That was a start. "I will agree to take the antibiotics if you will accompany me to dinner."

"No."

"I wish to thank you for your care and kindness."

"No. I don't date fighters."

"I no longer fight for Snook or anyone else. You were witness to my vow."

She pulled her hand from beneath mine, and I nearly groaned at the loss of contact. I couldn't wait long to make her mine. I needed to take her. Fuck her. Claim her.

She worked to keep herself busy tidying up and putting her supplies away.

"One meal. Please." At my words she stopped and stared at me. Her attention was like a gut punch. My heart pounded. My cock swelled.

She shook her head. "It's not a good idea."

"I am not a fighter. Not anymore." I leaned forward and lifted a hand to her cheek. I needed to touch her. It was a compulsion. Necessary.

Moving slowly, I ran my thumb along her cheekbone, down to her jaw. Her skin was softer than a flower petal. The softest thing I'd ever touched. "Please. I wish to thank you. I give my word of honor as a warlord you are safe with me."

"A warlord? What is that, exactly? Where are you from? I can't place your accent."

Fuck. I fumbled through my sex-crazed mind for the name of a country on Earth that might work to ease her suspicions. I'd studied her native language, the planet's geography and cultures. Their history, as much as I could take of it. Warlord? I was an idiot. "South Africa."

She raised one eyebrow and tilted her head to one side. "You're a long way from home, soldier."

"You have no idea."

She grinned as she wrapped her fingers around my wrist and gently lowered my hand away from her face.

"You can buy me a beer and a piece of pizza. The pizza place is two blocks from here."

"I accept."

"You asked me, remember?"

It was my turn to grin. "That is not how I will remember our first date."

"It isn't a date." There went that eyebrow again, as if she were scolding me. My fierce, fearless female. My cock jumped in my shorts, and I placed an arm across my lap to hide the evidence of my need for her. I was big, everywhere. The last thing I wanted to do was frighten her.

"You are correct." This was not a date. This was a claiming. After tonight she would never be alone again. She was mine.

She sighed and turned back to one of her cabinets. From the dark recess she removed a black bag nearly as large as my thigh and placed the long strap over her shoulder. "I have to go take care of Rico and Johnny. What did you do to them anyway?"

"I threw them out of the cage."

"You threw them?"

"Yes."

"Over the top of the cage?"

"Yes."

"That's hard-core. How much do you bench press, anyway? They aren't small men."

"It is not, as you say, hard-core. If I had been hard on them, they would both be dead."

The elderly driver, whom I had completely dismissed from my mind, snorted from the front seat. "He ain't wrong, Viv." He chuckled as cigarette smoke drifted from his mouth and nose. A foul human habit. "Too bad.

Killing 'em woulda been doing this neighborhood a favor."

"I do not kill for sport."

"So you said. What do you kill for then?" he asked.

I turned away from him to watch Vivian climb down from the back of the vehicle and walk toward the entrance of the fighting area. "For her."

Moving quickly, I fell in step beside Vivian.

She looked up at me, and I realized how very small she was. Fragile. Weak. A little, curvy, soft, gentle human. I would have to be careful when I fucked her. She looked...breakable.

"What are you doing?"

"Protecting you."

"I don't need your protection. No one in there would hurt me. They wouldn't dare."

So sassy, that mouth. And her assumption irritated me. The only one who could assure her safety in that hellhole was Snook. I did not want my female under his protection, nor his control.

She. Was. Mine.

Unable to stop myself, I reached out and wrapped my hands around her, just beneath her soft, curved ass. I lifted her into my arms, black bag and all, until we were face-to-face. "I am going to kiss you."

"You are?" Her eyes opened wide, and she appeared to be struggling for air, the two words barely there, more like a breathy whisper.

"Do you object?" I waited for her to choose. Now. Later. I preferred now, but I would not force nor frighten her. She needed to choose me and my beast.

We stared into one another's eyes for what felt like an

eternity but I knew was only a few seconds. She did not answer. Instead she leaned forward and pressed her lips to mine.

The move shocked my beast into silence. I held perfectly still, allowed my female to explore my lips. My mouth. I opened in blatant invitation. She hesitated, just for a moment, before her sweet tongue darted into my mouth.

With a groan, I took control. Her taste exploded on my tongue. Sweet. Seductive. Perfect. I pressed her close, the fullness of her breasts crushed to my chest, her hard nipples sending electric shocks to my cock. I could not stop. Could not get enough. She was everything.

Locking her to me, I lifted one hand to the back of her head and held her in place. Devoured her. Her tongue tangled with mine, her kiss aggressive. Needy. A soft gasp escaped her when I squeezed her ass, so I did it again and again. I wanted her naked and open and riding my cock. I needed her hands locked in place above her head, my mating cuffs on her wrists, my beast filling her, fucking her, claiming her for both of us.

I simply *needed*.

Moving slowly, I pressed her back to the wall of the parking garage, making sure to keep my arm in place behind her, cushioning her softness against the hard concrete structure. She lifted her legs and wrapped them around my waist, her pussy just out of reach of my cock. Clothes. We were wearing too fucking many clothes.

"Ah-hmm." Someone, a male, cleared his throat. Loudly.

My beast responded at once, whirling in place to

confront the threat with Vivian pressed to the wall behind me. Out of sight. Protected.

The old man, Wayne, had left his seat in the vehicle and stood near the back tire, watching us with a smirk on his face. "You two might want to do that somewhere else. One of them boys is bound to come out here looking for you. Wondering why you aren't in there taking care of their boo-boos."

"Boo-boos?" I asked. What the fuck was a boo-boo?

Behind me, Vivian sighed. "Oh shit. I completely forgot about Rico and John." She placed her palm on the back of my shoulder and patted me gently, as if afraid to anger me. "You better put me down."

I growled before I could stop the beast's response. "No."

"What do you mean, no?" There it was, that bite of feminine irritation. Her sass made me want to push her back to the wall again and fill that mouth with my cock.

"Do you plan to continue working for Snook when he forces his fighters to fight to the death?" I demanded an answer. Regardless of what she said, she would no longer be associated with that scum.

She shuddered. I had upset her.

Gently I set her down and pulled her into my arms, her cheek pressed over my heart. She resisted for a moment, then allowed me to hold her. Thank the gods.

"No. I don't know what I'm going to do, but no. I can't be part of that."

My beast settled, the urge to kill, to eliminate any and all threats to her, calmed. Although, I was so enamored of my female already, if she wanted to continue healing people, I would not deny her. She would simply need to do so elsewhere. Far, far away from Snook and his death matches.

"What is a boo-boo?"

"Their injuries," she answered.

Wayne snorted with disgust, and I agreed, liking him more each moment.

"Do you have a vehicle here?" I asked.

"No. I rode the bus."

Fuck. The idea of my female alone, at night, on one of the city buses made my entire body tremble with the need to kill something. "You will ride in my vehicle." I had one. I'd bought it after my first fight. The truck was old, ancient technology, but the motor worked and it gave me more freedom to roam in search of my mate. Now the battered truck would carry that mate to my home.

"Come." I held out my hand.

"I don't know. This is all so sudden. I don't even know you."

Wayne pressed something in his ear. "Yes, sir. She's on the way now." Wayne appeared to be speaking into thin air, but I knew Snook used primitive radio wave devices for communication. Wayne confirmed my thought. "That was Snook. He's wondering where you are. Rico is smearing blood all over the bar and laughing."

"God, Rico's an asshole."

I agreed with my female.

She looked up at me. "Okay. Let's go." She removed the shoulder strap from her body and tossed the bag toward Wayne. The black leather landed with a thud near his feet. "Stall for me?"

"Already done." Wayne grinned. "I'll tell him you got a headache."

"Tell him whatever you want. Just don't get into trouble on my account. And don't let Rico bleed for too long. He's mean enough already."

"Don't you worry about me, Little Red. Go. Take your wolf and get the hell out of here." Wayne tossed the envelope full of cash, my payment for tonight's fight, toward me. I caught it in midair and nodded my head in thanks. I'd left the envelope on the strange bed inside the vehicle, forgotten. Gods, this female was wreaking havoc on my system already.

"Go on, now. Both of you," Wayne insisted. "I'll patch up the assholes and give you a ten-minute head start."

Little Red? I found the name suited. She was small and had distinct red hair.

"Okay, but—" Vivian intended to protest.

No. I lifted my mate, tossed her ass up over my shoulder, and carried her into the night.

4

ivian

HOLY SHIT. Was I crazy? Had I lost my mind and all common sense?

What had I gotten myself into?

Maxus carried me over his shoulder like a caveman. I should have protested, but my lips were still tingling from his kiss. My entire body was nothing but melted butter trying to mold every one of my curves to Maxus's muscled frame. My core was empty. Throbbing. My nipples were still hard, taut peaks. I ached. For him. A stranger. And I had to bite my lip to keep from nibbling on his bare back. I had my hands in fists so I didn't reach for his ass beneath the shorts he was wearing. I wasn't angry, I was aroused, despite the fact that he refused to put me down.

I should have been outraged. Insulted. Not hoping he

would take me to his place and ravish me. "The pizza place is in the opposite direction."

"I know. You will not be safe there. Wayne heard you agree to accompany me on a not date."

Right. Wayne had been there, and Snook would be insistent. In fact, I'd probably want to avoid going home tonight, just in case. The last thing I needed was one of Snook's goons on my door in the middle of the night.

It had happened before.

Maxus walked nearly two blocks before stopping next to a truck that appeared to be at least twenty years old. I thought he would put me down. Instead he turned his head toward my ass and took several deep breaths, his body shuddering after each.

"You are wet for me." His voice was deeper, aroused.

Oh God. "What?"

"I can smell your pussy, female. I need to taste you. Now."

"Now?"

He opened the door to his truck and settled me on the edge of the driver's seat facing him, my legs dangling out the door. The truck was old enough that it had a bench seat stretched across the interior. Looking directly into my eyes, Maxus flattened his palm on my chest, just below my neck, and gently pushed me down. Down. When my back rested on the seat, he reached for the waistband of my pants.

So, now. He really did mean right now.

"Someone will see."

"You are mine. I need to taste you. Make you come." Had his voice become even deeper? I couldn't see all that well. The interior lights were old and dull, barely functional. Outside the door, his face disappeared in darkness and shadow. Hidden.

I searched for and found the dial that controlled the truck's interior lights. I twisted until the lights turned off to give us a bit more privacy. I wanted his mouth on me. His tongue inside me. Stroking my clit. I wanted to feel, not think. I did way too much thinking.

I reached for my pants and undid the belt and then the button at my waist. I pulled the zipper down. He watched as if hypnotized as I wiggled my hips, trying to pull my pants off. Once I had them over my hips, he took over, pulling them down around my ankles where they became stuck on my boots.

"Take. These. Off." I struggled to sit up, reaching for my boot laces.

"No." The deep growl made my pussy clench. Maxus lifted my ankles over his head, settled his face between my knees and spread my thighs wide, my wet heat on display and my ankles trapped behind his neck.

"Mine."

His voice rumbled through my body like an aphrodisiac, and my back arched up off the seat. He settled his palm on my bare stomach and held me in place with one hand as he slid a finger of his opposite hand deep into my pussy. His gaze was locked onto my face, watching me, my reaction to his touch. He looked at me like nothing else existed. God, he was intense.

He moved his finger, stroking my inner walls, hitting the sweet spot that made me squirm. Beg. I would beg this man for more. For release. For his tongue and his kiss and his cock.

He rubbed my insides again. Just. Right. I tried to

move. His heavy palm held my hips locked in position on the seat. All I could do was take what he gave me. Take. Beg for more. Wait until he decided to give it to me.

He lowered his lips and blew softly over my clit. Kissed me there. His lips touched down light as a feather, then were gone. Again. And again. When I thought my heart would explode out of my chest, he used his tongue. Tasted. Licked my clit. Stabbed deep into my pussy. Licked again. Sucked the small nub into his mouth.

Yes. God yes. "Maxus."

"My pussy." He lowered his lips and pressed a soft kiss over my clit as he slid a finger in and out of my wet core. "Mine."

I belonged to no one. But—damn. He felt too good to be real.

I wanted his mouth on me, and I didn't care if someone saw us. It was well past midnight. We were alone in a parking lot behind a run-down city building. And we were at least two blocks away from Snook's fights. If anyone was watching, so be it.

No one was going to mess with us. Maxus was a massive, frightening figure. As crazy as it sounded, I felt completely safe. Protected. Free to let go. And the idea that someone might see us was strangely...exciting.

I lifted my hips toward his teasing mouth. "Maxus."

"This is my pussy, female. You will come when I allow it."

The tone of his voice made the walls of my core convulse around his fingers. So hot. So damn hot. I was about to come.

"This is insane." My panting morphed into a groan as he slipped a second finger into my wet heat.

"Yes. Thank the gods you feel it as well." He sucked and flicked with his tongue, and I forgot all about trying to make sense of his words as my entire body bucked and fought to get closer to him. More. I needed more.

Using my legs, I pulled his head toward me as strongly as I could. I thought he would deny me. Thank God he smiled. "So greedy."

"Please. You're killing me."

His smile was pure male satisfaction as he lifted his head just enough to look up at me through his long, black lashes, his pale blue eyes so focused, so intense that I forgot to breathe.

"Already you beg." His deep voice made my pussy clamp down on his fingers. A moan escaped me, a sound I didn't recognize as my own.

"Please."

His smile was feral, his gaze that of a hunter. Intense. Focused. "Mine."

I wasn't going to argue. Anything, I'd promise him anything he wanted if he would just make me come. "Maxus."

"I am going to take you home with me, female. I'm going to lock mating cuffs around your wrists and secure your hands over your head as I fuck you. I am going to make you come over and over until you collapse from exhaustion." His hand on my stomach moved in a small circle, as if he were trying to comfort me as he revealed his plans. "Then I am going to feed you, bathe you, allow you to sleep, and then fuck you again."

Oh. My. God. *Please.*

The air left my lungs in a rush as my mind processed his words. Erotic images of him tying me up and having his wicked way with me played in my mind like a movie. I enjoyed a well-done pornographic movie. Except this time I would be the star. The sole focus of all his male attention.

Did I want that? Did I want him? His heat? His body covering mine? His cock buried deep?

"Yes."

The sound that escaped his throat was like a growl. Raw agony. Lust.

He lowered his lips to my pussy and fucked me with his fingers. Hard. Fast. He sucked and nipped and worked me until I exploded with a soft cry I had no hope of holding back. Maxus worked my body as my core pulsed, pushing me over the edge again before I'd had a chance to come down from the clouds.

I arched my back, tried to take him deeper. I reached for him with desperate hands, buried my fingers in his black and silver hair, and tugged. Held. Twisted. Pulled him where I wanted him to be.

When it was over, he moved backward so I could close my legs and slide back on the seat.

He moved into the driver's seat, his hair brushing the ceiling of the large truck's cab. God, he was big.

I scrambled to my knees and reached for him. I wanted to kiss him. Taste him. I wanted more.

"No, Vivian. If I touch you again, we will not leave this parking lot until dawn."

Well, that didn't sound so bad. But then again, that whole cuffs-and-tying-me-up thing had sounded fucking amazing. "Okay. Let's go."

He moved faster than any man I'd ever seen, positioning me where he wanted me to be. I was still naked from the waist down, my back pressed to his side as he closed the driver's door and started the truck.

I thought he would get us moving. Instead he looked me over, his gaze lingering longer and longer the lower his attention traveled. With a groan, he put the truck in gear and started driving. Once we were moving, he lifted his arm, covered my chest and abdomen with the heavy weight, and slipped his hand between my thighs.

"What are you doing?"

"I cannot stop touching you."

Damn, he was sexy. And I couldn't stop wanting him to touch me. I spread my thighs open, one leg pressed to the seat back while the other moved toward the dash.

He drove the truck out of the parking lot and onto the street. Seconds later two fingers slipped inside my wet heat, pushing in and out. He used his thumb to rub my clit as he drove. Each bump in the road, each turn or swerve made me gasp. He worked me until I thought I would scream, then backed off. Denied me release. Over and over.

I lost track of time, my mind a haze. My body was his now.

Giving in to his sensual play, I surrendered to him and to my own body's hunger. I was touch starved and hadn't realized the truth of it until he brought me back to life.

Could have been five minutes, could have been half an hour, I had no idea. The next thing I knew, he lifted me into his arms, cradled against his chest like precious cargo as he carried me inside his home. The house was small and run-down, needed some paint. That was the only thing I saw before we were inside.

He gave me no chance to look around. His lips were

on mine the moment we entered. His hands tugged at my boots, his large fingers surprisingly deft at untying my laces and dropping my boots to the kitchen floor. My pants followed. He carried me down a short hallway to a bedroom and sat me on top of a king-size mattress, a soft blanket under my sensitive skin. The muted light from the kitchen spilled through the open doorway. The light had to first travel through a short hallway, and the bedroom was barely more than shadows and darkness.

"Arms up," he ordered.

I lifted my arms, and he slipped my shirt off over my head. His gaze dropped to my bra, and his chest heaved. "It's red."

"I like red, even though it's not in my color wheel."

"I love red." He dropped to his knees before me, leaned forward, and pulled one nipple into his mouth, red lace and all.

I loved red, too. Especially in his mouth. My fingers were buried in his hair, holding him to me before I was conscious of the movement. He laved attention on the other breast as well, making me lift my chest toward him in encouragement. If he wanted to play, I would play all night. I needed this. I'd been alone a long time. Responsible. Always working. Working. Working. Worrying about everything and anything. I deserved a hot-as-hell one-night stand.

The bra needed to go. Now. I needed his lips on bare skin.

Seconds later I had the clasp undone and I tugged the straps down my arms. I tossed it onto the floor.

I thought having me completely naked would move Maxus along. Instead he leaned back on his heels and looked at me for so long I began to think he was having second thoughts.

"Everything okay?" I asked.

"Perfect. You are even more beautiful than I imagined." His tone was a deep bass that rumbled through me like a physical caress.

I wasn't all that beautiful. I had red hair and a few freckles. Skin so pale every blemish looked like a fire ant on my skin, and I was more than a little overweight. I was curvy, to say the least. Very curvy. But he was staring at me like I was a goddess come to life, so who was I to argue?

"Then why did you stop?"

He stood slowly and then walked to the small nightstand next to his bed. Opening the top drawer, he pulled something dark and metallic-looking out and turned to me.

They looked like wrist cuffs. Not handcuffs like the police used. More like really wide bracelets.

"What are those?"

"I told you I wanted to tie your arms over your head and fuck you, make you come over and over until you collapsed from exhaustion."

Oh, yeah. *That.* "I remember."

"These cuffs will secure your hands. I will wear a matching pair."

"Am I going to tie you up, too?" Kinky. I liked the idea of having all that man to explore and tease at my leisure.

"No. Not tonight." He grinned again, and the look made him appear almost boyish. "Perhaps, if you are very, very good, I will allow you to have your way tomorrow."

"Tomorrow?"

He walked back to me and knelt between my knees. "One night will not be enough. Not for me."

Was this guy for real or was he playing me? Telling me what he thought I wanted to hear? I'd already said yes; there was no need to lie.

Whatever. I was tired of worrying. Analyzing. *Thinking.* I was an adult. I was going to take tonight and enjoy myself. No strings. No expectations. Just sex.

Hot, kinky sex with the most gorgeous man I'd ever seen.

I held out my wrists and waited, surprised when he latched the very large set of cuffs around his wrists first. He shuddered as he locked the second one in place. A soft groan left his lips, and he lowered his head as if he needed time to adjust. I wasn't sure if his reaction was from pain or anticipation.

"Do they hurt?" I was not into pain.

"They will not hurt you. I give you my word."

What did that mean? They hurt him? I looked down between his legs, and there was no hiding that huge erection under the fighting shorts. So either they didn't hurt, he was into pain, or he was about to lose control.

Reaching out, I pulled one of the smaller cuffs into my hands and ran my fingertips along the smooth metal. They appeared to be what he said. Simple metal. No barbs or spikes or anything weird that would hurt my skin. I wrapped it around one wrist and watched, fascinated, as it seemed to close itself and shape to my arm. "Wow. That's weird. Where did you get these?"

"From a friend."

The complete absence of anything that looked like a

locking mechanism made me nervous. Were they magnetic? "How do you take them off?"

He froze, his shoulders tight, head bowed low so I could not see his face. Gently he took my wrist in his hand and ran a finger over a small indentation I had not noticed before. At once the cuff released, and so did the nerves threatening to strangle me. I locked the cuff in place and removed it again, just to make sure I knew how to do it.

I was about to allow a complete stranger to have me at his mercy. Once I was cuffed and restrained, I would have no control. None. What if he wanted to hurt me? What if he didn't stop when I told him to? Or kept me chained to the wall for hours and hours, refusing to release me?

What the hell was I getting myself into?

Maxus had my other hand in his now, his touch gentle. Reverent. Like I was a delicate flower or breakable china. He looked into my eyes, the second cuff ready. "May I?"

Oh fuck, fuck, fuck. Was I going to take this chance? Risk giving him this much control?

"Yes."

He shuddered. The slight movement moved through his entire body as he slipped the cuff onto my wrist. Again it seemed to close on its own. Strange, but they felt fine. I wasn't sure how he thought he was going to use these to tie me up, but I figured I'd find out soon enough. And the thought made my pussy clench and my nipples harden. A shiver of anticipation rolled over my skin, making me cold and hot at the same time.

"Are you going to tie me up now?" I was smiling,

trying to keep things light, fun, sexy, but even I could hear the raw need in my voice.

Maxus's body trembled and shook. He dropped to his hands and knees on the floor in front of me, his face down.

"Maxus?"

"Mine." He growled, actually growled like a wild animal. I scrambled backward on the bed with a giggle, away from him. Apparently it was playtime at last.

He loomed up over me, nothing more than a shadow in the dark. His hands came down on either side of my knees.

"Mine. Your pussy is mine. Your wet cream is mine. Your skin is mine." He tugged on my ankles, moving me closer and closer to him until my bottom was on the very edge of the bed.

He lifted me into his arms and carried me around the bed to the far side of the room.

"What are you—" My back pressed to something soft. Padded. There was a small seat anchored to the wall, and Maxus set my bottom on the edge of some sort of ledge.

"Hands over your head."

I trembled and did as he commanded. Once I raised my hands, he gathered both of my wrists in one large palm and moved them up higher on the wall, closer together.

I felt the moment something caught the metal and held me in place. A magnet? A bracket? I had no idea, but I was laid out for him like a virgin sacrifice. My breasts were bare and thrust forward. My legs were spread wide, Maxus standing between them, the slight ledge I sat on just wide enough to cup my ass and thighs and keep my pussy open and on display.

Moving slowly, he eased each of my feet into a molded rest along the wall so I could lift my bottom if I needed to adjust. I wasn't doing the splits, but I was more exposed than I was used to. Open. Naked and hanging on the wall like a painting. I was his and my pussy wept for him. I'd never been so turned on in my life.

Maxus leaned down, rested one of his hands on the wall next to each of my hips, and licked my pussy. Once. Twice. He kissed his way up my abdomen to my breasts and sucked. Licked. Rolled with teeth and tongue until I gasped. His palms pressed to my inner thighs, stroking. Petting. Teasing my core with his thumbs. Pulling my flesh apart, opening me for his cock.

"Are you ready for me?" He pushed two fingers deep. Three. I wanted to scream at him to hurry. I'd had an orgasm. My pussy had been wet and throbbing for what felt like hours. Was I ready?

"Yes. Fuck me."

"I want to watch you come." He leaned in close and pressed his forehead to mine. Our gazes locked as he moved his fingers in and out. Harder. Faster. "Then I'll fuck you."

I moaned. My eyelids drifted down. I was so close already. So close...

"Open your eyes. Look at me."

The order pushed me higher. The room filled with the sound of his fingers fucking me. In and out. Wet. Hard. He worked my clit with his thumb and I lost control.

The orgasm rushed through me like a blowtorch

lighting every nerve ending in my body on fire. All that teasing. Edging. Bringing me to the brink but not allowing me to have an orgasm on the drive here. Now I exploded, the spasms moving through me from the tight curl of my toes to my shuddering lips. The walls of my pussy clamped down on his fingers, pulsed around and over his touch. And all the while, my gaze remained locked to his. I could not look away from the dark pools of his eyes. The light from the hallway spilled around the back of his head like a halo that made him seem other-worldly. A god. A fantasy come to life. I could not deny him because to do so would be to deny myself.

"Maxus." His name was a demand, nothing less, as he pulled his hand away from my core and removed his shorts.

"Mine."

I felt him then, the rounded head of his cock pressed to my entrance. I wiggled, trying to get him inside me. Closer.

Slow, steady pressure. His cock thrust forward, spreading me open, stretching my pussy to the brink of pain. I couldn't hold his gaze any longer. He leaned forward, pressed his body to mine, skin to skin. Cock buried deep. We were one.

My neck arched, my body convulsing around his hard length as another orgasm rolled through me at his inva-sion. So big. So deep. God. So good.

A soft sob escaped me as he bottomed out inside me. Pulled out. Thrust deep. Faster this time.

"Mine."

He had a one-track mind. Not that I minded. His primitive, possessive role-playing made me hotter. I was tied up, trussed to the wall like an offering to a god. He was my god tonight. My sex god. God of pleasure. "Mine, Maxus. Tonight you're mine."

His lips traced the skin of my arms as he moved inside me. His chest heaved as if he struggled to maintain control. He growled in the dark like an animal, a beast. The sound made me crazy with lust. I had to be out of my mind. Too many orgasms. My brain had to be nothing but a hormone pool at the moment. I was losing all rational thought as he pumped into me, his huge cock filling to the point of pain...then pleasure. He was so big. Strong. Fierce. Protective. His shoulders completely eclipsed the little bit of light coming in from the hallway. I felt like I really was his. Possessed. Desired. And totally safe.

"I..." He uttered one word. Pulled out. Pushed his cock In. Hard. Deep.

"Yes." More. I needed more. "More."

As if his body was listening, his chest filled my vision. My lips pressed to the center of him. I breathed him in and instantly became addicted to his smell. My core burned, then settled, my body on fire. Literally I couldn't get enough air into my lungs. Couldn't get enough of him. His scent. His heat. His cock.

I pressed forward, pulling against the restraints so I could taste him. Lick his chest. Nuzzle his skin with my nose. Caress him with my lips.

God, was his cock getting bigger?

"I am." He rolled his hips. Nibbled at my skin. The shudders that racked his body pulsed through my pussy and my flesh as if they were my own.

"More. Please. Don't stop." I was begging now. Fine. I

didn't care. I nipped at his skin, licked him to lessen the sting. I couldn't stop, couldn't control myself. He was so good. So much. So deep inside me.

"Yours. I am yours."

Could he get any sexier? Any more perfect?

No. Impossible. Every taste, every thrust made me need another. "Don't stop. I need more."

He responded to my demands, pumped in and out of my body like a machine. His growl became a rumble. Louder, like a wild beast in my ear. The sound of him losing control pushed me into a third orgasm. I bucked and thrashed on the wall, but his body was too big. The cuffs too strong. I could not move, only take what he gave me as he thrust into me over and over.

My orgasm stretched, each movement of his huge cock hitting my nerve endings, pushing my buttons, making me gasp and shudder and lose control as my pussy fluttered and ached, pulsed and shot pleasure through my body.

He came with me at last, the pulsing of his cock, his rigid arms and shoulders, his loud shout of pleasure somehow making my own orgasm even more intense. Longer.

He was going to kill me with pleasure. That was what I decided when I finally came back into my body. I opened my eyes to find him staring at me like he wanted to devour me. Worship me. Like I was the most important person— the *only person*—on the planet that mattered to him.

Too intense. Too much. I couldn't hold his gaze, not after what he'd just done to my body. I was feeling vulnerable and exposed and way out of my league. I'd had sex before. I'd even had babies. I wasn't an inexperienced virgin. But nothing had ever been like this.

Not even close.

He owned me now. I felt possessed. Obsessed. I'd never been the kind of woman to give a man anything he wanted just because he was good in bed. I'd never understood women who couldn't stand up to a man and just tell him no.

But Maxus? What would I be willing to sacrifice for more of this? More of *him?*

The answer scared me...a lot.

"Are you going to let me down now?" My voice was raspy. Broken. Weak. Just like I was feeling.

His cock remained inside me, buried deep. He moved, just a slight shift of his hips, and I gasped. He was growing inside me. Already hard again. Ready.

He moved slowly, deliberately teasing me as his hand slipped between our bodies and he found my clit with his fingertips. Rubbed. Slow. Fast. Slow.

"Oh God." Just like that, I was on the edge. So sensitive. So swollen. Every cell in my body under his command.

"Not your human god. Maxus. I am Maxus."

I would have laughed, but he moved his fingers again and my body shuddered, completely out of my control. "Maxus."

He took my lips in a kiss as he fucked me again. Pumped into my body where he had me pressed to the wall. Played with my clit. Made me beg.

"Mine, Vivian. I've been looking for you for a long time. So long. I'd given up hope."

"What?" Why was he talking when I had no hope of concentrating on his words?

"Mine. You're mine." He thrust deep. Kissed me like he needed me. Couldn't get enough. Was desperate to taste me. Claim me. Protect me. Devour me.

Like I was important. Special. Adored.

All beautiful, seductive lies. But for tonight I took his body in mine, gave in to pleasure and pain. Lust and need. And chose to believe.

5

M axus

DARK RED HAIR. Her eyes, hidden by soft skin and long lashes, were a fascinating mixture of gold and green. With the lightest touch I could manage, I traced the adorable brown speckles that dotted her nose and cheeks. Dawn was long gone before Vivian stirred in my arms. I had not slept, my beast and I both fighting disbelief that we had found her, our mate. She was real. She was beautiful and soft, her body curvy and accepting of my hard angles and inhuman strength.

Her eyes fluttered open, and she tilted her chin to look up at me. "Good morning."

"Good morning." And it was, the best in my living memory. Vivian's cheek rested in the dip of my shoulder, her leg thrown over my thigh as if she were afraid I would escape. We were both naked, warm, and clinging to one another beneath the sheets. If she knew how tightly I needed to hold her, she would run from the monster rattling around inside me, the beast demanding to break free. Touch her. Fuck her. Claim her.

Using every ounce of will in my body, I held the beast in check. She was not ready for him. She would run. He would chase her and kill anyone and anything that got in his way. As was our right, on Atlan. On The Colony. Fuck, anywhere in Coalition-controlled space. But not here. Earth was not a full member of the Coalition of Planets. The truth about what was out there was still being spoon-fed to Earth's population so as to avoid panic. They would not understand the true terror of an Atlan beast lost to mating fever. I must act as one of them. A human. An average human male falling in love with a female.

Inside my mind, my beast growled and raged, fighting me. In agony. The fever stole his control and all rational thought until all he could think about was *her*. Fucking her. Protecting her. Giving himself to her, his strength, his power, his seed. All hers for the taking. A shudder ran through me, and Vivian grinned up at me with a warmth in her eyes that made me weak.

Not. Yet. I scolded my beast, and myself. This deception was dangerous, for both of us. Yet I did not have a choice. Vivian thought I was a man. A human whose anemic emotions could be twisted and turned, my devotion given and taken away.

I was Atlan. My beast would kill to keep her, protect her, claim her. There would be no other female for me, ever. She was mine and I was hers. Vivian was all that stood between me and insanity, the deadly effects of mating fever. Execution.

She was the only living being who would be able to control my beast. Tame him. Lure him. Appease him. Her voice. Her touch. Her soft skin and wet pussy. The full, soft roundness of her body pressed to mine.

I had to woo her, make her love me, before I could reveal the truth about what I was. An alien. A warlord from another planet. A scarred soldier. A killer.

"Cold?" She moved, lightly rubbing the palm of her hand over my chest. I shuddered again, this time with awareness. Need. My cock stirred at the small attention she bestowed upon us, desire becoming need when she repeated the motion.

"Hungry." For her.

"What time is it? We haven't had breakfast."

"Not for food. For you."

Her hand stilled on my chest as if my words had shocked her.

Lifting my free hand, I traced the curve of her cheek with the back of my fingers. So soft. So fucking perfect for me. "You are so beautiful."

Her cheeks and neck turned pink, and she tried to turn her face from mine, lowered her gaze.

"Look at me."

She did so, but her entire body had shifted from relaxed to tense with those three words.

"You. Are. Beautiful."

"You. Are. Delusional." She smiled as she insulted me. "But thank you."

I would never escape her, nor her me. We were one now. I would protect her. Worship her. Care for her. Fuck her and give her pleasure. Anything she required, I would provide. She. Was. Mine. My beast agreed, even as he raged to break free and claim her himself.

Not. Yet.

My mating cuffs were on her wrists. My beast, whom I had restrained last night, had fought hard for freedom. Thank the gods, when he roared the loudest, I was already buried balls-deep in our female, my cock sinking into her wet pussy, her scent filling me with contentment. Belonging. Peace.

Fucking peace.

I could not remember the last time my beast had been so quiet as in that moment. The constant agony of mating fever had faded for a few minutes, leaving me to feel like a normal male giving pleasure to my female, enjoying everything about her.

I had been gentle with her, as much as I could be. Careful. She was small and fragile. Kind. A healer. I admired her for being one of the humans who served others by darting around in the vehicle with lights. The humans called the vehicle an ambulance, and they served humans, taking care of people who were injured or sick. I could kill, rip enemies to pieces with my bare hands. I did not heal.

With a sigh, she snuggled closer. "I guess I should get going."

"Where do you believe you need to go?" I could not bear to be parted from her. My cock agreed. I was hard. Ready. Eager to fill her again and again. All fucking day. Over and over...

"Well, I have laundry to do. My girls are coming over for dinner tonight, and I don't have anything to cook. It's

Saturday, which means I need to put the trash down and water my plants. You know, the usual."

I knew very little about human routines, and nothing about hers.

That was something I needed to change.

"I would like to meet your daughters."

She pulled back and looked up at me again. "What?"

"I would very much like to meet your daughters. With your permission, Vivian." Her name on my lips felt like a caress. "They are important to you, and so they are important to me."

"Whoa. Don't you think we're moving a little too fast?" She sat and pulled the sheet up to cover her luscious breasts.

I tugged the fabric down and twisted to take one nipple into my mouth. When I could smell her arousal, I moved to the opposite breast with a stop in between to kiss her on the lips and answer her question. "No. Not fast enough."

Her laughter turned into a moan as I moved my hand between her legs and explored. "You can't... I mean, we can't..."

I kissed her again, tugged her onto the bed so she rolled onto her back. I moved so that her body was laid out like a feast beneath me, and settled my hips between her legs. Kissed her again. Nuzzled her neck. She smelled like heaven to me. Perfection. Indescribable and perfect.

"Can't what?" Holding myself over her so as not to bury her under my weight, I shifted until the tip of my erection aligned with the entrance of her core.

"You are so bad." She ran her hands up and down my chest, petting me, the mating cuffs on her wrists a visual

reminder of our bond. My mate. *Our mate*. My beast practically purred.

"I am very, very good."

She laughed, the sound healing something inside my
soul that I'd believed damaged beyond all repair, and
lifted her hips, took the tip of my cock inside her body.
"Yes. That, too."

I pressed into her slowly, gave her time to adjust. She
was wet and ready, but I was large and she was very, very
small compared to an Atlan female. Probably still sore
from last night's claiming. And this was a new position.
I'd kept her on the wall last night, desperate to control my
beast. Like this, I would press her into the mattress, thrust
so deep her body rocked forward and back on the bed as
I filled her. Fucked her. Claimed her again.

"Mine." Poised over her, I looked down into her eyes
in the light of day, made sure she knew I meant what I
said. "You're mine, Vivian."

"You're a neanderthal."

"I'm a beast." I shifted my hips and thrust deeper.
Harder. Filled her completely and held myself in place
with her pussy wrapped around my cock, her body
pinned to the bed under my hips, and her gaze locked on
mine. She. Was. Mine.

With a soft moan, she arched her back, moved her
body against mine, fucked me as I held perfectly still
above her. After a few moments she wrapped her hands
in my hair and tugged in frustration. "If you're a beast,
you should act like one."

"Should I?"

"Yes. Right now."

"Now?" I moved in and out of her body just enough to

drive her mad. "Like this?" I pulled out nearly all the way. Pushed deep. "Is this what you want from your beast?"

"Yes. Tell my beast I need at least two orgasms before we get out of this bed."

Lust raced up and down my spine like an electric current running from my ears to my cock. *My beast.* I nearly purred like an animal at her casual claiming.

"Anything, female. All you need do is ask."

————

MAXUS, Vivian's Apartment, Dinner

"MOM! OH MY GOD." Stefani, Vivian's oldest daughter by eight minutes—or so I'd been told—had followed her mother into the kitchen to help with the dishes. At least that's what she'd claimed as her intention. Both females had waved me off when I began to help. I had been living on Earth for months. I knew how to use soap and a sponge, and I did not expect my mate to serve me in such a way.

In fact, I would very much enjoy feeding her the next time we were alone. I would make her lick my fingers after each bite. Perhaps choose something sticky, like caramel or melted chocolate. I had learned from various advertisements that human females very much enjoyed such treats.

"Well? Mom? What the heck is going on with him?"

"I know, right?" Vivian's happy laughter flowed through the kitchen into the living room, making my beast settle deeper into her couch. They had no idea that my Hive implants allowed me to hear every whisper.

"He's hot," Stefani said.

"Very."

The silence stretched, and I met the gaze of the female who remained seated across from me, Adrian, Stefani's twin sister. Adrian was much more reserved. Quiet. An analyst. She would be much more difficult to win over than her sister. And I must impress them both, assure them that I would make their mother happy. Because when she came with me to Atlan, or The Colony, her offspring would need to know their mother was safe and happy.

Something banged against the counter. "You're blushing. You had sex with him! When? When did you meet him?"

"Last night."

The young female sitting across from me in the cushioned recliner crossed her arms and frowned at me like I had offended her. The other two continued to rant in the kitchen.

"What? You just met him and you already slept with him? This is so not like you. And what's with those medieval bracelets? It's weird. He's weird. I don't like this. Why him? You haven't dated in years, and you start out with a fuck boy like that?"

I did not care where my female had been in the past or which males she may have been intimate with. They were irrelevant. She was mine now.

As to the term *fuck boy,* I was no boy, but I definitely knew how to fuck my mate until she screamed.

"I don't know what got into me. He's just so..." Vivian's

voice faded softly as she searched for a way to describe her feelings for me. I leaned forward, eager to hear anything she might reveal.

"Big?" Stefani prodded. "He's practically a giant."

"Yes, but..."

"Sexy?"

"Yes, of course. But there's just something irresistible about him. He's so..."

I couldn't stop the smile creeping across my face at the wistful note in Vivian's voice. With Vivian's other daughter, Adrian, watching me like a hawk, I made sure to cover my smile with a hand over the lower half of my face.

"So what? What, Mom? How old is he? Is he single? Divorced? Does he have kids?"

"I don't know."

"You didn't ask?"

"No."

"Oh my God! This is a disaster. Where is he from? Is he a fighter? Please tell me he's not one of Snook's fighters. Those guys are all either batshit crazy or drug addicts."

"He's not a drug addict."

"How do you know?"

"I just know."

"So, he's batshit crazy then."

"No."

"Gambling debt?"

"I don't think so."

"A drug dealer? A washed-up boxer? Is he stupid? Does he even know how to read?"

"That is enough, Stefani."

"But—"

"Enough!" Vivian's voice had taken on a tone I had not heard from her before, one used to being obeyed. My beast preened at the sound of her anger, eager to tangle with her. Dominate her. Transform her anger with pleasure.

"Mom, this is crazy. Come on."

I had heard enough as well. I stood—slowly, so as not so scare Adrian—and cleared my throat. I spoke loudly, made sure my voice would carry. "You will not speak to your mother with such disrespect, Stefani. You are a child. Your mother is a mature female who has taken care of you and made sure you were not injured nor starved as you grew into adulthood. She is your elder and deserves deference and respect."

Both females came out from the kitchen and stopped once they rounded the corner to face the small living room. Vivian's gaze met mine, and there was heat there. Acceptance. She was pleased I had spoken on her behalf.

Good. She would not be treated with such disrespect while she was mine. Which meant no one would be allowed to speak to her in such a tone ever again.

Stefani, however, had her hands on her hips and her mouth partially open as if I had shocked all words from her body. "Excuse me?"

"You will apologize to your mother, now. And then you will both leave."

"What?"

Adrian stood slowly and wiped her palms on the thighs of her jeans. "You are being a little bitch, Stefani. It's Mom's life."

"I'm trying to protect our mother, thank you very

much." Stefani glared at me like I was a Hive Integration Unit about to contaminate her entire family.

Adrian walked to me and held out her hand. "It was nice to meet you, Maxus."

In keeping with human tradition, I took her hand in mine and moved our joined hands up and down several times. Odd tradition, but not difficult to learn. "You as well, Adrian, daughter of Vivian."

"See? He's weird." Stefani moved across the room to join her sister, and they stood shoulder to shoulder, inspecting me.

They were dressed in nearly identical clothing. Tight jeans, boots with high heels, shirts made of a stretchy material that hugged their shoulders and breasts. They were well-formed, beautiful females. I did not doubt they had many human males fighting for their attentions.

"How much do you spend on your hair?" Stefani asked.

"I do not understand."

"You know, the color? What's that cost? Two or three hundred a month?"

"My hair costs me nothing. It grows from my head without expecting payment." I looked at Vivian, confused. Had I missed something so fundamental about humans? Did they pay hair specialists to force their hair to grow? How odd.

"That hair is not natural," Stefani insisted.

She was correct. My hair had once been so dark as to be nearly black. But the Hive had changed me on a cellular level. The gray had begun to grow in place as the torture went on and on. The silver had come later, with more integrations. After every treatment, the three colors changed, rearranged themselves until now I had this mark of shame, of weakness on my head.

Of failure.

"I think it's the sexiest hair I've ever seen." Vivian's gaze was fixed on my head, and her eyes were round and soft, sincere. "I love your hair, Maxus."

Stefani threw up her hands. "You're impossible, Mom. I give up." She turned to me. "And you really are weird. Sorry to be rude, but I don't want my mom to get hurt."

Both girls had their mother's green and gold eyes. Where Stefani's hair was a dark brown, Adrian's was a vibrant red, just like her mother's. Their faces and forms left no doubt of who their mother must be. All three females were beautiful. And, I realized, all three were now under my protection. These younglings were untrained and wild. Naive. Foolish. Easy prey for males without honor. Were they on Atlan, I would not be as worried. No Atlan male of worth would ever harm a female. However, a fair number of human males were reckless, foolish, and had not mastered their own urges. They were primitive and did not always honor nor respect their females.

In short, they lacked self-control, discipline. Honor. And I wanted no such males near my new daughters.

"I would never hurt your mother. I would die to protect her...and you. She is safe with me."

"Everything you say is so strange," Adrian finally said to me, but her words were not a judgment, merely an observation. There was no ill will behind them, nor blame. Simply curiosity.

I allowed them both to stare but held out my hand to Vivian, urging her to join me. She moved at once, gliding toward me with a smile as I pulled her tightly to my side where she belonged.

"Is strange a bad thing?" I asked.

"The jury's still out," Adrian said. She took her sister's hand and pulled her toward the door. "Come on, Stef. We need to get back. We told Carmen we'd meet her at nine so we could hit Greg's party."

Vivian followed them to the door, where all three females hugged one another several times and said their goodbyes. When they were gone, Vivian closed the door. Turning around, she leaned her back against the painted metal and looked at me.

"Well, that went well."

"Did it?" I walked to the door and placed my palms flat so my body surrounded hers. I needed to breathe her in. When her hands lifted to my chest, my beast practically purred.

"Your ears aren't bleeding, so I'd say the evening was a major success." Her grin was contagious, but her presence, the cuffs she still wore, her easy acceptance of me in her home all combined to humble me. She was a miracle, and she had no idea how perfect or special she truly was.

I leaned in close and held my lips just above hers. "I need to kiss you."

"You do?"

"Yes."

"Need?"

"Yes. I need to taste you."

"You are too sexy to be real." She lifted her hands to my neck and combed her fingers through my hair. "Why me? I'm nobody, Maxus. I don't have family or money. I'm not beautiful or interesting or—"

I cut off her protest with a kiss meant to let her know she was everything to me. She was my family. When we returned to the Coalition, I would be rich, should I choose to accept the gift from my people. The Atlans took care of their warlords, those that survived. Most Atlans returned home to wealth and lands. Those that went to The Colony did not need such things and either declined or passed the riches to a family member.

I wished to return home. I would be wealthy. Respected. I could provide my mate with anything her heart might desire. And right now, I desired her. She was the most beautiful female I had ever seen. Soft. Curved. Perfection.

Before I realized what was happening, I had my arm under her ass and her back pressed to the door. My lips on hers. I took and she melted under the onslaught of my need. I could not get enough. Her scent lured me. Her kiss drugged me. The softness of her body felt like heaven. Nothing had ever felt as good. Nothing.

My cock sprang to life, hard as a rock in seconds. She rubbed her body against mine, just as eager. Needy.

She tugged at the buttons of my shirt. When her shaking hands proved inefficient, I ripped it from my body with my free hand, groaned in an agony of need when her small hands touched my shoulders. My chest.

"This is crazy. Why are we so crazy?"

I reached beneath her skirt and pulled the barely there scrap of fabric aside to expose her pussy. There wasn't much to the lacy fabric, a small triangle over the front and a thin string of fabric up the back. I'd watched her put them on earlier and fantasized about removing them nearly every moment since.

Her breath came in short gasps, and the scent of her arousal filled the small space between us. My beast wanted to roll in it, take the wet heat from her core and rub it all over her body so I could taste it everywhere. Her lips. Her breasts.

My beast fed me images of devouring her pussy with our lips and tongue, taking our time, feasting...

I slipped two fingers inside her, and she broke the kiss, her head turned to the side as she moaned my name.

Nothing had ever made me feel more complete. I belonged to this female, heart and soul. She was mine. I was hers. I was enamored. Addicted.

Her core was hot. Wet. She was ready.

"I need you."

"You use that word a lot."

I pushed my fingers deep. Rubbed her clit. Claimed her lips again and again. "I *need* to fuck you."

"Again? Oh God." She lifted her legs to wrap her ankles around my hips. "Yes. Fuck me. Do it."

Fuck. Yes.

I tore open the human pants I wore and freed my cock. She wiggled until the tip aligned with her pussy's entrance. I didn't need another invitation. I thrust deep.

Her fingers wrapped around tendrils of my hair and pulled, lighting my body on fire with her urgent demand. She tried to lift herself, to ride me.

I lifted her body, dropped her on my cock. When I had enough of teasing her, I held her in place and fucked her hard and fast, her back to the door. Her orgasm rushed through her in a matter of minutes and my long-abused, scarred body was all too eager to follow her into release after so many years of pain. Torture. Battle. War.

My seed pumped into her, marking her with my scent, my claim. My beast fought to be free, to join the fray, to claim her in my true form. I held him back. Human. I had to pretend to be human or I would frighten her. Lose her.

Half-clothed, we panted, our bodies locked together. I lowered my lips to the top of her head and held myself still, my kiss pressed to her soft hair, her body still surrounding my cock, claiming me for her own. The heavy metal of my mating cuffs became more a part of me every time I touched her. I would never take them off. Should she need to be away from my side, I would gladly suffer the painful reminder that I belonged to someone. That she accepted me. Fucked me. Made me hers. There was nothing I could ever do to her that would be enough to care for her, to reward her. Nothing would ever be enough to honor her. I wouldn't just die for her, kill for her...I would destroy worlds.

"Maxus?"

"Hmmm?" I moved so that my cheek rested against the top of her head, shifted slowly so that my chin, lips, and jaw caressed her in turn. I could stay like this forever. She was so small, so light in my arms. Her feminine smell hypnotized me. Her shampoo. Peaches? Some type of fruit? So sweet. Addictive.

"Maxus?"

"Hmmm?"

"Are we going to stand here all night?"

I smiled, wrapped my arms around her, and carried her with me, away from the door. I settled on the couch, her on my lap. My cock slipped from her body as she adjusted herself into a comfortable position. She straddled me, our combined scents making my beast want to rumble with satisfaction. I told him to shut the fuck up. Vivian didn't know about him yet, and I didn't want to panic her. I needed her to be addicted to the pleasure we gave her before I revealed the truth.

I'd seen enough human movies to know that in most, the aliens were monsters. Killers. Creatures to fear. Why the human governments distributed this view of others, I had no idea. Other than the Hive, most advanced societies were far more civilized and compassionate than the humans dreamed to be. There were good and bad among all species, but on Earth the divide appeared to be growing. Rich. Poor. Nations. Religions. Us and them. There would be no peace on this planet until the people grew to understand they were all one in their place in the universe. One planet. One people. One.

The Hive would not stop at an arbitrary line drawn on a human map. They did not make deals nor sign treaties. They were impossible to influence, bribe, or corrupt. In that way, they were more than the species they integrated into their society. I had fought to be free of them. Killed them, in fact. But I'd been one of them for a long time, and I understood how they thought.

There were no individuals in the Hive. Well, few. Very, very few. And I had no desire to dwell on the Nexus unit who'd fought for control of my mind for so fucking long. Not with my mate sated and sitting on my lap, her eyes still glazed over with desire. Contentment.

She leaned in close, and I wrapped my arms around her as she settled against my chest. "You make me crazy, you know that? What am I going to do with you?"

"Wait a few minutes, crawl down to the opposite end of this couch, and allow me to fill you from behind?"

Her small hand landed with a slight thump against my chest. "Stop that."

"Never. I will never stop wanting to fuck you."

That earned me a squirm. She leaned back, way back, against my arm. "Look at me, Maxus."

I obliged. How could I not? I looked down at my stunning mate and waited.

"You sound like you mean that."

"I do."

She shook her head, the movement of her silky hair a caress against my arm. "You're impossible. You've only known me a couple days. Less than that, actually."

For once I was happy to borrow a human phrase. "When you know, you know."

"And you know?"

"Yes."

"What do you know, exactly?" Her eyes narrowed and I sensed I was on dangerous ground, although I wasn't at all sure how I had arrived in such a precarious position with my female.

What did she wish for me to say to her? I had no idea. The beast paced within, restless and on edge. He felt it, too. We were being lured into some kind of trap.

"Maxus?"

Fuck. "I admit I do not know much about you, Vivian. But I want to learn. I wish to know everything about you and your life. Every detail."

She laughed. "Oh, you're smooth."

"I am not smooth. I am hot, remember?"

With a sigh she settled her cheek against my chest

once more, and I heaved a sigh of relief. "What do you want to know?"

"Tell me about your daughters and their father." I needed to know if he would make a claim of his own, if she cared for him.

"Go for the jugular. Okay." She took a deep breath as if the memory was painful. "When I was fifteen, I thought I was in love. He was popular. Cute. He had a nice car, and I came from nothing. We had sex, terrible, painful, awkward sex in the back seat of his car. Two months later I had a positive pregnancy test and his parents moved him across the country. His father was a lawyer. When I told him I didn't want to terminate the pregnancy, they had me sign some papers saying I would not put his name on the birth certificate and never come after him for child support. He told me if I tried to find them, he'd have a judge take the baby away from me. I signed. They left and that was that. Probably stupid, but I didn't want him in my life anyway. I had the girls when I was sixteen. He's never seen them, and they don't want anything to do with him."

"Sixteen is very young."

She shrugged. "My mom had me when she was fifteen, so it was an improvement on the family legacy. She was also working and helped me out. We lived with her until the girls were fourteen." Her voice quivered. "Then Mom...couldn't stick around anymore."

"I do not understand."

"She smoked her whole life. Lung cancer got her. It was quick."

I did, indeed, know of what she spoke. Cancer was an unnecessary plague on humanity. "I am sorry."

"She tried to hang on, but the chemo wasn't working so she decided to just stop treatment. She left me everything she had in her checking account, and we've been on our own ever since."

"You are alone?"

"No. Well, I wasn't. I had a brother, too. My twin brother, Fabien. He joined the military the day he turned eighteen, did ten years, came home a few times here and there. He sent me a text message that he was going to join the Coalition Fleet. He was big on *Star Trek,* you know? He signed up, and I haven't seen or heard from him in years. The girls don't even remember him. I figure he's dead."

"No. If he had been killed in battle, you would have been notified."

"How do you know that?" She twisted in my lap, trying to look me in the eye. I avoided eye contact by lifting my hand to touch a strand of her hair. I could not lie to her, but I had spoken out of turn, revealed too much.

"Is that not the way of all military operations? If a warrior is killed, they notify the warrior's family?"

"Warrior?"

"Soldier."

"Yes. I guess. But if he's not dead, I don't know what the hell happened to him."

"Perhaps you could send in a request at the processing center. It is just a few miles from here, in the city."

"Oh, I know exactly where that place is. They took my brother from me. No thank you. That place is cursed.

And if I ever meet one of those aliens, I'm going to tell him to go to hell."

Everything in me stilled, my beast cold and silent. "The Coalition is protecting Earth."

"From what? I haven't seen any proof of anything out there. I think it's all bullshit and lies. They take human women for their bride program and pay out money for them like they're buying slaves. They take the soldiers and pay nothing. And for what? What are they fighting? They never have anything on the news about the aliens and their war. No pictures. And where is all the amazing technology we should have? Like medical gadgets and lasers and stuff. A cure for cancer? Genetic treatments to cure all inherited disease? I don't even know what the aliens have, but I can smell a lie a mile away, and the entire Interstellar Coalition is full of lies and more lies. They don't respect Earth at all. They just take and take and take."

"Your brother did not share this view?"

She shrugged. "I don't know what Fabien thought. I think he wanted to be Luke Skywalker or Captain Kirk. I think he didn't know what he was getting into until it was too late." She sighed and lifted herself so she could kiss me. "Why are we talking about this when we could be doing something much, much more interesting?"

Before I could answer, she lowered her still-wet pussy onto my cock, her wet heat sliding over me like a glove. I was still hard for her. Aching. I doubted that would ever change.

I let her have her way, lifting and lowering herself on my lap, taking me at her leisure. Her head fell back, her neck exposed, her soft moans of pleasure like electric jolts that went straight to my cock.

How would I ever reveal the truth to my mate. I was everything she despised. An alien.

A liar.

Did she truly mean what she'd said? Did she hate the Coalition? Would she blame me for the loss of her brother? If I told her the truth, would she hate me as well?

I searched my memories, examined every moment of my time on Earth, and realized Vivian was correct. There were no reports about the Hive war. No technology had been shared with the humans. No S-Gen machines, ReGen healing, transport capabilities. Nothing dangerous.

I thought of the humans screeching at the fight club, nearly apoplectic in their screams for blood, violence, and killing. The Coalition had refused to give the humans anything they could misuse. Which was...well, everything.

Vivian fucked me, took me deep over and over. I stared at my mate, the only female who could save me, and decided I would live as a human. Forever. She did not need to know the truth, not if it meant I might lose her. I would fuck her in the dark, allow my beast to claim her just once, in the blackest of night. Bind him to her. Cure the mating fever. And I would stay here, on this planet with Vivian for as long as she would have me.

Going home to Atlan meant nothing without her. If living as a human would make her happy, allow me to keep her close, then that was what I would do.

She settled low across my lap, my cock buried deep in

her pussy, and lifted her hands to run her fingers through my hair. I groaned with pleasure. Gods, her touch was magic. Heaven.

Bliss.

"I have a surprise for you," she whispered.

"What is it?" I whispered back, happy to play her game.

"I have a set of bright red lingerie." With a sexy grin, she slipped off my lap, my body instantly and acutely aware of her loss. "Stockings. Garters. It's sexy and I haven't had a chance to wear it."

"I like you naked."

"You are such a man." She laughed and stepped backward, toward her bedroom. "Do you want to play a game?"

Gods help me, I could not deny her. Nor did I want to. I hadn't played for so long I wasn't sure I remembered how. "My answer will always be yes."

Her happy laughter made my beast surge forward, desperate to touch her joy, share this moment. I held him back by sheer force of will, desperate to keep Vivian content and unaware of the monster I truly was.

Her voice was husky and strained. "I'm going to put on my red lace, Maxus, and you are going to play the part of the big, bad wolf."

"What does this bag, bad wolf want?"

"To eat me."

Fuck. Yes.

She ran her tongue over her lower lip to entice me and I had to fist my hands at my sides to stop myself from reaching for her to drag her back.

"Vivian?"

She wiggled her eyebrows as she giggled like a wild thing. *My wild thing.*

"My, my, my, what big"—she lowered her gaze to my exposed cock, the eager fucker still rock-hard and straining toward her—"teeth you have."

I began to rise from the couch, but she held out her hand to stop me. "No. Not yet."

I thanked the gods for years of disciplined military training as it took every ounce of control I possessed not to follow her into her bedroom, bend her over, grab her by her hair, and fuck her from behind for her sass.

I fucking loved her sass.

It was only a few minutes later when she emerged in a complete ensemble of dark red lace and satin, each piece strategically placed to lure me to her body, drive me mad with need. Matching high-heeled shoes completed the look.

I was going to fuck her in those heels. I wanted to feel their sharp points digging into my hips and ass.

"You're the big, bad wolf and I'm the innocent young lady simply trying to bring you some cookies." She posed. Stretched. Bent over. Ran her hand over her curves and cupped her breasts. She had been accurate. Stockings. Garters. Another barely there thong panty that exposed the round globes of her perfect ass. I had seen such things in human advertisements, never understanding their power—until now. "Do you like cookies?"

I removed my clothing as she stared, her chest heaving, the sweet musk of her arousal impossible to miss as her body called to me.

She held my gaze until I stood naked. Ready.

A growl escaped me and she smiled. "Should I run?"

"Yes." Gods, yes. "Run, Little Red."

With a squeal she raced for the kitchen.

The apartment was not large, and I caught her seconds later. I spun her around so that she faced away from me and pressed her lace-covered breasts to the cold countertop. I gently moved the strip of red lace that covered her pussy to one side and slid my cock deep. Thrust hard. Once. Twice.

Grabbing her thick hair in one hand, I angled her head up and back, toward me. "Did you think you would escape the big, bad wolf?"

"When are you going to eat me?" she taunted.

With a soft swat on her perfectly round ass, I pulled my aching cock free, then leaned over her to whisper my command in her ear. "Run."

She ran, her joyous laughter making me smile as I followed, caught her, fucked her. Brought her to the edge of orgasm. Let her go.

"Run, Little Red. Run."

She raced for the living room. This time, when I caught her, I sat down on her couch and lifted her body so that her thighs rested on my shoulders. Her feet dangled down my back. Her hands tangled in my hair, clinging to me for balance as I feasted on the wet pussy I held to my mouth.

"Maxus—"

I didn't answer for a long, long time.

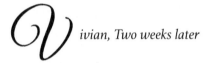

ivian, Two weeks later

I KNEW Snook was going to be angry that I'd left the fights last week, angry that I didn't show up on time to work the fights tonight. Just...angry. But not *this* angry.

"Goddamn it, Vivian. Get your ass in the car. We're going to the club. Now." He paced along beside me where I walked on the sidewalk outside of my apartment. His large black SUV rolled next to me like a shadow, the windows tinted so dark I couldn't determine if Wayne or someone else was driving him tonight. He sat in the back seat, window rolled down so he could speak to me.

"I quit, Snook. How many times do I have to tell you that?"

"Don't make me force you. You're one of mine and have been for a long time. Don't fuck it up now, Vivian. Don't fuck it up now by making me even more angry."

"I'm not trying to make you mad. I just can't play nurse at the club anymore."

"Why not? What changed? Other than that bastard you let into your bed?"

Was that jealousy in his voice? Surely not. He was more like a disturbed uncle to me, never someone I would ever consider dating. After spending the last two weeks floating around in a cloud of Maxus pampering me and a seemingly endless supply of orgasmic pleasure, dealing with a raging lunatic felt like someone had poured a bucket of ice water down my shirt.

"I quit, Snook. I told you that. I told your boys that when they called. I told Wayne when you sent him down to my work—which was not okay, by the way. I can't work for you anymore. I quit."

He took a long drag on his cigarette, the glowing tip nearing the filter. He held the smoke in, twisted the cigarette butt around in his fingers, and then tossed the still-burning end onto the ground directly in front of my feet.

I crushed it under my shoe and kept walking.

"You left Rico and John bleeding."

"You said they could wait and Wayne told me he'd take care of them."

"I don't need Wayne, I need you. He doesn't have your training."

"There are other nurses out there. Doctors. Paramedics. Thousands of us."

"But they aren't mine. You're one of mine. This block is mine. These houses are mine. These streets are mine. You feel me? You're mine. Your girls are my girls. You don't get to quit."

What. The. Hell?

I stopped moving, and the SUV rolled to a stop with Snook's open window right next to me. He leaned out the vehicle's opening, trying to be close, to intimidate. I took a step toward him so that our noses nearly touched and held his gaze. Bastards like him never responded well to fear, so I showed none, despite the fact that my heart raced, my lungs burned, and I could barely think straight. No one messed with my girls. I had enough street in me to be very, very bad if I had to be.

"I don't want a misunderstanding here. Are you threatening my girls? Is that what this is?" I would kill him. I would fucking kill him. I didn't know how, but if he touched either one of them, he would die, and I didn't care what happened to me after. Life in prison? Fine. Torture by his cronies? Whatever. I would *end* him.

He took his time. His breath reeked of gin and cigarettes. "My girls. You got that? This is my fucking town, and you don't get to quit on me."

"I told you, I'm done. You want those fighters to kill each other, fine. But I won't be part of it."

"You owe me. Who kept a roof over your mother's head? Huh? You think those bills just vanished all on their own? Who put food in your belly when you were hungry? Who helped feed those two brats of yours, huh? Your mother understood how to play the game. Guess you don't know the rules. Allow me to clarify. I owned your mother, and now I own you. All three of you."

"Leave my mother out of this."

"Would, if she didn't still have ten large on the books. Someone needs to pay that debt."

"You're lying." Even as I said the words, I knew he was

telling the truth. I loved my mother, God rest her soul, but she had never been perfect. She had her weaknesses. Trusting men with power was one of them. And Snook always had plenty of power in this city.

"I never lie about money."

Shit. That was true. Everyone who grew up here knew it, too. That was one of the reasons he had managed to stick around for so long. He was hard, but he was our kind of hard and you always knew where you stood with him.

"Ten thousand?"

"Since she's dead and all, I'll waive the origination fee."

"Why did you give her so much?" What the hell had my mother done with that kind of cash?

Snook tilted his head, and the look in his eyes wasn't cruel. "Something about paramedic school. Uniforms. Daycare. Ring any bells?"

Every bit of fight drained right out of me. For me. She'd borrowed money for me. My tuition, uniforms, daycare for the girls because they'd still been too young to stay home alone... God. This was my fault. I sighed and took a step back. "Shit." I whispered the curse under my breath.

Snook reached inside somewhere and pulled out a fresh cigarette. Lit it up and sucked the smoke in like it was pure bliss. "We had a thing, you know, for years. I always considered you a daughter."

I was going to throw up. But he wasn't lying about his relationship with my mom. I knew she had spent time with him—slept with him, let's call a spade a spade —from time to time. I never asked her for details because I didn't want to know. I still didn't want to know.

"Snook, I'm sorry. I can't do it. I can't help you out anymore. Not with the new direction the fights are taking." I wasn't going to spell out my suspicions that his fight club was heading in the *kill club* direction. "I'll make payments or something."

"No. Nothing's changed at the club. Nothing. I had an idea, you know, but it didn't work out. The big wolf man you're fucking these days made sure of that."

"Excuse me?"

"Sorry. *Making love.* Is that better for your sensitive little ears?"

How my mother had ever been attracted to this man was beyond me. Incomprehensible. No orgasm could have been worth putting up with Snook's bullshit.

Snook raised an eyebrow and stared me down. "Fights start in two hours. No one's dying, Viv. You have my word. Be there."

Shit. Shit. Shit. I had no choice. "I'll be there, but take my cash and use it to pay down what my mother owed you. Six more months and I'm out."

He grinned at me. "Six more months and we'll see." He leaned back, disappearing inside the big black vehicle. He nodded to the driver, and the car rolled away as the dark window rose to hide its occupant once more.

Six months. Goddamn it. Snook would try to figure out a way to keep me around. I would try twice as hard to make sure he didn't stand a chance of succeeding.

I had two hours. That was not even close to long enough for what I had planned with Maxus for tonight. I had dinner—and dessert—all planned out. We were supposed to go to his place tonight. And he'd promised to let me wear those cuffs again, try out that perfect ledge in his bedroom.

My body tingled with anticipation. "Down, girl. You aren't getting any action tonight. Damn it." Spending time with Maxus was just about the only thing I looked forward to these days, other than my mandatory weekend dinner with the girls. If I didn't force them to come home from their wild college life to see their mother, I wasn't sure I'd ever see them again.

Not true. They were amazing daughters, but why take the chance?

I pulled my cell phone from my pocket and found my man's number. Guess we'd just have to postpone our date.

———

Maxus

THIS WAS NOT ACCEPTABLE.

Crouched low on the three-story rooftop, I stared at the text message stream on my human cell phone, irritated with the primitive device.

VIVIAN - HEY BABY, I have to work tonight.

- *I will wait. What time do you get off?*

Vivian – I'll be really late. Not at the station. Tomorrow?

. . .

REALLY LATE? Not working at the fire station? Then who—

"Fuck." I nearly crushed the device in my hand. Snook. It had to be Snook.

I answered her because I needed her to know I would be waiting for her. Always.

I WILL BE THERE to drive you home. The last fight should be over by midnight.

Vivian - How did you know?

You are mine to protect.

Vivian - That is not an answer.

I am fighting tonight.

THAT HADN'T BEEN part of my plan, but with Vivian committed to being at the fight, I could not leave her unprotected. To safeguard her, I had to get inside Snook's club. The only way to get inside and walk around without half a dozen of Snook's assholes shooting their guns at me was to fight.

VIVIAN – Of course. S is an asshole. Be careful.

Be ready to kiss me and make it all better.

MY COCK GREW hard at the thought of what I would do to my female after the fight. There was no danger to me in the fighting cage. These human males were small and weak, even for a warlord without Hive enhancements.

With them, I could take on several of my own kind and defeat them. The Hive had made me a monster, a creature to be feared. The only thing that stood between my beast and the rest of the world? One very sassy, incredibly sexy female. If I lost her now, before my beast had fully claimed her, there would be no hope of containing my beast or the mating fever. Even with the Hive integrations to assist, I would be lost. Truly lost. I would rend and tear. Destroy everything and everyone in my path. Kill without mercy or remorse.

I could not lose her.

VIVIAN – I have another surprise for you.
Is it red?

PLAYING *Little Red* and the *Big Bad Wolf* had become one of our favorite games. I had already asked Vivian to wear the enticing red lace outfit three times since that first night. My cock jumped at the thought of chasing her, bending her over, snarling in her ear like a wolf, pumping in and out of her hot, wet pussy. My mind filled with a haze of need, the mating cuffs on my wrists shooting pain through my arms and shoulders barely enough to ground me to the here and now, even as I monitored the movement of the Hive Tracker team in the building opposite me.

Snook. The Hive. Me. So many threats to my female, and all I could think about, obsess about, was filling her with my cock and making her come, making her cry out with pleasure, making her mine.

This was dangerous. Every rational cell I had left in my body recognized the fine edge I walked with my beast. I would have to take the risk and allow him to claim her. Soon. As soon as possible.

Tonight, he growled inside my head. I didn't argue. I could not. The threats to our mate required his protection as well as mine. I could not risk her life. If the Hive were to track her down, I would need to unleash my beast to defeat them. I would no longer have a choice.

They were close. They were here. I could not wait, not even until morning.

I glanced back down at the cell phone to read Vivian's response to my question. Red lace? Blue? Black? Perhaps white with small ribbons and bows I could untie with my teeth. Since the first night I had taken an interest in lingerie. I wanted to fuck my mate while she wore everything. All of it. Remove the clothing and fuck her some more. Maybe she would wear green and gold to match her eyes...

Vivian - If I tell you, it won't be a surprise.
If you tell me now, I'll give you an extra orgasm.
Vivian – Behave.
You don't mean that.
Vivian – True. See you tonight.

I GRINNED. Gods, I was totally in love with my mate. She was perfect.

I was not surprised to learn that Vivian would be at the fight club this evening. Just a few hours ago, Snook had threatened to kill me if I didn't fight tonight. I'd told him to go fuck himself. He'd smiled at me, said, *See you tonight,* and walked away. I didn't know what he had planned, but I was not shocked he'd used Vivian to get to me. A mate was a weakness, a pressure point. Normally I would remove Snook's head from his body without a second thought. On Atlan, his threat to my mate would be just cause for his death.

Here? On Earth? I had to follow human laws or risk everything. Forced transport off world. Leave my unofficial mate behind. Risk losing her. I knew she was a dedicated mother. She would not want to leave her daughters. That devotion and care was one of the reasons I had grown to love her. Passionate. Playful. Fiercely protective of her daughters. Loyal. Strong. A healer. There was so much to love about her, so many reasons I was not worthy of her.

I was a liar, an imposter, an outcast, and a fugitive all in one. I did not deserve her. And yet I would kill anyone who tried to take her from me. Anyone. Anything. Human or otherwise.

That included Snook, but he was a problem for later.

These Hive motherfuckers sneaking around in the old brick building across the street from my residence?

They had to die. Now.

Moving silently, I jumped from the adjacent rooftop onto the building currently occupied by Hive Trackers. They were undoubtedly setting up surveillance using information transmitted to them from the last batch of Trackers I had disposed of.

Gods be damned, I should have moved to a new dwelling when the previous trio of Hive Trackers had discovered my home, but part of me had relished the hunt. The danger. My beast *wanted* to make them pay for everything they had done to this body over the last few years. *Wanted* to be found. *Wanted* to fight and kill and destroy as many of them as possible.

I could not allow the beast to rule me. Things were different now. I had a mate, a female to protect. A family. Her stubborn, innocent, protective daughters were now mine. My family. My mate and children. Mine.

Horrible timing to discover more Hive Trackers were here, hunting for me. By the gods, I was tired of this dance. They tracked me without ceasing. Five times since my initial escape, I had been forced to eliminate an identical threat, always three Trackers working together. Once they were dead, I would have a few weeks of peace. Silence.

Then the buzzing would begin again, a faint tingle in the back of my mind. The closer they came to me, the louder the annoying buzz became until I could hear them every waking moment. I listened to the muddled sound of them talking even now. Connecting. Working toward their one unified goal—to find me and bring me back to the Nexus unit that considered himself our father, in a way. He controlled our collective consciousness, a cluster of thousands of minds, of Soldiers, Integration Units, Trackers, and Scouts.

And me.

That blue fucker wanted to regain control of me. I was still part of him, part of his collective.

I wasn't sure exactly where I fit into the Hive hierarchy. Even among the Hive, I'd been singular. Unique. Not a mere Soldier. More than that. The Nexus unit had spent extra time on my integrations, placing new, experimental designs in my spine and at the base of my skull, under my skin. The integrations had attached to the bone itself and multiplied, spread like an infection until the biosynthetic implants coated the inside of my skull and spinal column, ran along the complex web of neurons inside my brain and body. The Nexus unit had told me that the integrations would control my beast and lessen the effects of the mating fever.

At the time, not only did I not care, I'd been eager to die. To forget. To end the torture.

The Nexus had proven correct. Without the integrations, I would have been long dead. Even now, with the sharp pain the mating cuffs caused where they circled my wrists, that pain, the reminder that I had a mate waiting for me, depending upon me, would not have been enough. The usual control mechanism used to calm generations of Atlans would have failed with me. The fact that my beast had not yet claimed Vivian for himself was just part of my current problem.

When the Hive finally captured me, I'd been too far gone, my mating fever too advanced. Without the Hive integrations, I would already be dead. I should be dead.

"Fuck." The truth twisted inside me like barbed wire. I should be dead. I deserved to be dead. I had been captured when I should have fought to the death. I had killed the Hive reconnaissance party the Nexus unit had sent to Earth. Once I'd broken the mind control and killed them, I should have killed myself, not wandered around for months trying to find a female like Amanda Bryant, Commander Zakar's human mate.

She had intrigued me, even then. I had never seen a

human female before, and she had been fearless, passionate, protective. A highly intelligent warrior. She had stood toe-to-toe with Grigg and Conrav, defied them, submitted to them. Dared to love them.

I had never seen such a female, and I became obsessed. Despite the fact that Amanda and my Vivian looked very different on the surface, the shades of their skin and hair, their eyes—one dark and one golden—their hearts held the same strength and devotion.

If I were dead, who would protect Vivian from Snook? From the savage males on this planet? From the Hive who, even now, scouted and schemed to take human females for purposes unknown.

That was a lie. I sighed. I knew exactly why Nexus Six wanted a human female—to breed. To save his unique race.

Crouching low, I took up position just behind the rooftop door and sent out a call to the three Trackers just one floor below. They would come to me like bees to honey, as the humans would say. I did not hate them, nor did I hate Nexus Six. But I could not allow them to infiltrate Earth any more than they already had, and I feared their presence was already beyond the Coalition's ability to eradicate.

Slow seconds seemed like hours as the three Trackers moved inside the building and up the stairs toward the roof. Toward me. Getting closer.

Closer.

When the door to the roof opened, the three stepped forward as one, walking with complete synchronicity in their movements, each step and turn of the head in perfect parallel to each other.

I allowed them to move to the center of the small area before closing the door behind them. As one, they turned to face me, and I assessed my enemy.

Two former Prillon warriors and one blue male from Xerima. All three incredibly strong, fast, and deadly.

The nearest Prillon spoke, his gold-toned skin not possible to mistake for human. "Beast, we require you to accompany us now. Nexus Six wishes to speak with you."

I rose to my full height, my beast clawing at my gut to break free, his insistence physically painful. "I am not part of the collective. I am not Hive."

All three Trackers closed their eyes at my denial and remained unmoving, as if speaking to one another—or Nexus Six—directly.

This was new. The last batch had attacked the moment I spoke to them.

The Xeriman male opened his eyes first, his gaze dropping to my wrists. "You have claimed a human female." The two Prillons, the golden one and the other, who had a dark skin tone similar to human coffee, both looked at me, one set of eyes golden, the other copper-hued. Focused. *Interested.*

Fuck. I should have taken off the cuffs, but the thought, even now, was abhorrent to me. I belonged to Vivian. These cuffs marked her claim on me, my belonging, my purpose. I was hers.

"No."

"You wear Atlan mating cuffs. We can smell her on your skin." The blue male took a deep breath as if to emphasize the point. "She will breed."

"No."

The dark Prillon looked at me and raised his weapon,

an ion blaster particular to the Hive. "Nexus Six demands we acquire the female. Where is she?"

"No!" My beast roared through me, and for once I did not try to hold him in check. I welcomed the agony of shifting bones, swelling muscles, the increase in blood flowing through my limbs.

I had no ion blaster, but I would not need one. I was Hive. I was Atlan. I was a beast unlike anything before.

I rushed the Xeriman male, the largest of the three, his teeth, claws, and tough skin the deadliest threat. He could rip my throat out with his bare hands if enraged, nearly a match for my beast, and I had no idea what enhancements the Nexus unit had ordered special for him.

So close, the heat of his flesh warmed my palms, an agony of fire ripped into my side, and I fell to one knee. *What the fuck?*

The golden Prillon heard my thought, so close we were once more linked, mind to mind. "Nexus Six created a new weapon. We are pleased to discover it is effective."

The dark Prillon held the weapon pointed at my head. "Where is your female?"

"Fuck you."

The Xeriman's mind pushed into my thoughts, ripping through my head like he was carving my brain into pieces with a scalpel. "There is a competition among males. She will be there."

"No!" Ignoring the pain, I leaped toward the Xeriman, my hands on either side of his skull. I would crush him like a grape.

Fire. Agony. The Prillon fired his weapon again, but I did not loosen my grip. Squeezed.

The blaster pressed to the side of my head, at my temple. "Release us, beast, or we will kill you and take your female."

Their ploy might have worked had they been speaking to me. My beast had no rational thought, nothing within but killing rage. He intended to protect his mate at all costs.

I stopped fighting him, gave him free rein. The Xeri-man's head imploded, the bones of his skull crunching and collapsing between my palms as if made of saltine crackers. I dropped his lifeless body to the rooftop.

With a roar, I turned to face the two remaining Prillon warriors.

They both took a step back, raised identical weapons.

They would kill me. So be it. I would be damn sure to take them with me. No one was going to touch Vivian. Especially not the Hive. Not Nexus Six.

The first shot hit me in the chest, and I stumbled, kept walking.

The second hit my hip. I fell to one knee. Got up.

The third hit me in the face.

7

axus

THE BLAST FORCED my head back, the snap causing the bones in my neck to crackle as they struck one another. I turned toward my attacker, my beast roaring so loudly car alarms went off on the streets three stories below.

"Increase the strength of the blast," Golden Boy ordered.

"We are not to kill him," the darker Prillon argued.

They were arguing, each thinking independently of the other. Without their third, the Xeriman, the connection between their minds must have become weak.

Each male adjusted their weapon as I fought to get close enough to finish this fight. A stronger blast and they might take me down.

That was not acceptable.

A silent rumble moved through my chest as if a large

truck approached at high speed. Alarmed, I looked around for another threat.

Atlan warlords leaped onto the roof, appearing as if from the shadows. Five of them. Six. They surrounded the Hive Trackers and roared with me. I recognized Velik, the Atlan who worked as a guard at the Interstellar Brides' Processing Center. Another, Bahre, I recognized from the television, from the program featuring exiled males from The Colony trying to find mates. The other Atlans I did not know, but they focused on the Hive Trackers, not me.

Allies.

My beast barely registered the thought before charging the two Hive Trackers.

They stepped close together and vanished into thin air, the body of the Xeriman male disappearing as well.

"Transport beacons. Fuck." The warlord named Bahre cursed, and my beast agreed. Bahre had claimed a human female. He wore mating cuffs. The other males' arms were barren. Unclaimed. No female had found them worthy. Not yet.

I stopped my charge, my beast enraged that the enemy had escaped. He wanted to fight. To kill.

My roar shook the rooftops, and I heard several windows break.

"Knock it off, Warlord, or we'll have the human helicopters and those fucking police snipers trying to take us out again." Bahre stepped toward me, either the strongest among them or the most foolish. He looked fierce, scarred. I recognized in him a fellow Atlan who had suffered. Greatly.

"Trackers." My beast was still in control, and he didn't feel like explaining.

"No shit." The Atlan closest to Velik stepped forward. "They've been buzzing my brain for days now. We've been hunting them, but every time I get close, they disappear." He held out his arm in a warrior's greeting. "I am Tane."

I took his arm in a warrior's greeting, my beast somewhat eased by the presence of other warlords. "Maxus." The moment we touched, I *heard* his mind and I understood. "They can hear you, as I can. That is why you cannot catch them."

"Shit. I was afraid of that. I can't turn their noise down any further." He rubbed a hand through his hair and looked at one of the others. "Maybe Dr. Surnen can figure out a way to take it down a notch when I get back to The Colony."

"If you go back," Velik said. "I want to see what Bahre's lady, Quinn, comes up with. This Cinderella ball sounds promising. Beautiful, available females everywhere, all eager to find a mate. I do not want to miss it." He looked at me. "And I'd rather not get killed in the meantime by Hive Trackers who aren't supposed to be on this planet."

Bahre walked toward the place the Xeriman's body had been as I released Tane. "I didn't think the Hive could control Xeriman warriors. Their minds are too chaotic, too wild. We need to let the war council on Prillon Prime know about this. Xeriman warriors in the Hive could cause problems. I wonder how many they have? How long they've been taking them?"

"Two hundred and four." I wrestled my beast back

under control so I could speak clearly. I had to protect Vivian. To do that, I had to be able to *think*. That was the only argument the beast had accepted. He wanted Vivian protected, too. At any cost.

"What?" Bahre's gaze snapped to me.

"Two hundred and four Xeriman warriors had been integrated at my last count. I do not know how many years the Nexus units have been working on integrations capable of controlling their distinctive minds."

"So, Maxus, who the fuck are you and what are you doing here? You have integrations, but you're not from The Colony." Tane's gaze wandered up and down my body, what he could see of it around the human jeans and T-shirt I wore. "I can't see your integrations, but I can feel them."

"You can hear the Trackers as well? Is the sound clear enough to follow them?" I needed to kill those two Prillons before they could get to Vivian.

"Yes. I can hear them and I can follow, though not if they have transport beacons. They could be anywhere on this planet, or any other, by now." Tane motioned with his arm to include Velik, Bahre, and the others.

"I will contact Warden Egara and ask her to scan for unusual transport activity," Velik offered.

"They won't leave without me." Nexus Six wanted me back under his command. And now, apparently, he wanted Vivian as well. If he had my female, I would do anything to protect her, to spare her pain. I would be his pawn in truth.

"Why does he want you?" Bahre stood a few steps in front of me, his arms crossed over his chest, his mating cuffs a reminder to me that he was not my enemy.

Tane's gaze did not leave my face. "I assume they were hunting you, specifically."

"Yes."

"Why?" Bahre asked. "And why are they here? They should not be here. Earth is too far from their base of operations and has no weapons or other assets. The males are plentiful but much smaller than other planets equally vulnerable. This does not make sense."

"They're a tracking unit, sent by Nexus Six to recover me."

"They want you? Just you?" Velik asked.

I nodded. "For now."

"I smuggled the ReGen wand and mating cuffs to you because I thought you were an honorable male. You lied to me. You were not here with the others." Velik tilted his head to indicate the other warlords surrounding me on the rooftop. They had come to Earth through diplomatic channels, their presence here approved and monitored by the human government. They were even participating in the television program designed to make males from The Colony more appealing to human females. "How did you get to Earth?"

"I came here as an active Hive Soldier."

Every single one of them took a step backward and assumed a fighting stance.

"And where are the other Hive now?" Bahre asked.

"Dead."

Tane stood up straighter and studied me as if he could discover my secrets just by looking. "You broke their mind control and killed them."

"Yes."

"Why didn't you leave this planet? Go straight to the

processing center? Report the Hive incursion to the Coalition?"

I held up my arms, mating cuffs clearly visible. "I had to find my mate. I could not leave at that time. I would have been executed immediately."

"That bad?" Bahre asked.

"Yes." I would not lie, nor deny how close I had been to the edge, not to these warlords who had suffered as I had. Fought in the war. Been captured. Tortured. Integrated.

Escaped.

I had watched—and laughed from the safety of my dwelling—as the first warlord walked off the human, Chet Bosworth's, stage and chose a female, took her to a side room, and made her scream with pleasure as the humans had scrambled to control the situation. Control *him*. Warlord Wulf, if I remembered correctly.

Their second attempt had not fared much better, the male lead being replaced at the last moment because *that* Atlan, Warlord Braun, had mated to a random female working at the hotel where the warlords had been staying.

And then there was Bahre, the giant staring at me. He had very publicly mated with a human female who worked as a news anchor here in Miami. He had requested special permission to establish a domicile here and been granted that permission for two reasons, as I understood it. One, his wealth—humans were very impressed with possessions. And two, he was to be an official ambassador to Earth along with his mate, his *wife*. To fit in with human customs, he had claimed her in a human ceremony called marriage.

I knew their stories, and I had stayed away from them all for a reason. I was not supposed to be on Earth. I was a danger to human and Atlan alike, to the entire purpose of their television program. No female would be willing to take an Atlan mate if they saw one ripping humans to pieces, wreaking havoc, creating chaos with rage and indiscriminate killing. That would have been me without Vivian, and without the enhanced integrations provided by Nexus Six.

The six warlords stared at me in silence, and I knew they would wait hours for the information they needed. Mainly information about me.

"I am Maxus. I served with Battlegroup Zakar in Sector 17 until I was captured. I spent more than three years in the Hive Integration center, the favored experiment of Nexus Six. I was sent here with a group of six to establish a forward operating base for Hive surveillance and breeding programs."

"Breeding programs?" Tane asked, horror in his tone.

Bahre's bellow of rage set the car alarms off again, and he grew in size, his beast rising to the surface to protect his mate. I knew he would try to kill me now if he thought I was a threat to his mate, the human female whose face I often saw on television, Quinn.

I held out my hands, palms forward. "I killed them all, Bahre. Every single one of them and a dozen Trackers since."

When I was certain Bahre was not going to charge me, I lowered my hands slowly. "The two Trackers who were here broke into my mind and discovered that I have a mate. They took the information from my memories and will try to take her tonight."

"As a means to control you," Velik mused.

"Yes."

"We will assist in the hunt and kill the Trackers, help protect your mate," Tane vowed.

I looked at the others who stood behind Bahre, Velik, and Tane, the Atlans who had remained silent the entire time. "And who are the rest of you? Why should I trust any of you near my mate?"

Tane lifted a hand and pointed to the three warlords in order. "These warlords are Iven, Kai, and Egon. They survived the Hive and are from The Colony. They are honorable males. They came here with me and the others as possible subjects of the *Bachelor Beast* television show."

I snorted. "That hasn't worked out well so far."

Bahre laughed out loud. "Not for the human television producers. For some of us, it has worked out very well indeed."

Tane nodded at Bahre. "His mate, Quinn, has promised to organize a large gathering of females to an event called a *Cinderella Ball*. Quinn believes we will all find our mates at this event."

I lifted a brow. I knew of this human fairy-tale story, *Cinderella*. I had been on Earth long enough to absorb some of their culture, especially where it pertained to female interests. I was an eager and apt student of human females' wants and desires. Being swept off their feet by a prince seemed to be atop every unclaimed lady's list. "You do know that Cinderella runs away at midnight. She escapes her mate, and no one knows who she is."

"What? How are we supposed to claim a female who

runs away? Is this part of the event? Surely not." Tane looked at Bahre, who shrugged.

"Ask Quinn. I know nothing of her plans. Nor am I familiar with the story."

"When is this ball?" I asked.

"In three weeks," Iven offered. "Until then, we wait."

"Well then, Warlords, I welcome you to my hunt." I took my cell phone from my back pocket and checked for messages from Vivian. There were none. I was simultaneously disappointed and relieved.

"Where do we go now?" Bahre asked.

I looked at each of the warlords in turn. Every one of them was a true Atlan giant, a head taller than even the tallest human males. They wore human-style clothing, as I did. Walking alone, we might fool the humans, appear to be one of them. Together? I was not sure there was any type of clothing on this planet that could truly hide what we all were. Aliens. Warriors.

Beasts.

"We go to Miami Snook's fight club. I am expected to enter the cage tonight. The Trackers will be there as well, as that is where my mate will be."

"You are expected to fight? With humans?" Tane sounded shocked and disgusted by the thought.

I shrugged. "I have been here many months, alone. I needed human money to survive here. I have procured a home and a vehicle. The humans involved pose no threat to me. In fact, I am always careful not to kill one of them accidentally."

Iven moved from the shadows behind Bahre into the light from a nearby streetlamp. "You are speaking their language."

I nodded. "Yes. I learned quickly. It was necessary to survive. The human females do not have NPUs to translate Atlan. The women Quinn brings to the ball will not have NPUs either. How did you plan to speak with any of them if you have not learned their language?"

NPUs, short for Neural Processing Units, served as universal translators for any bride or fighter in the Coalition. However, the guests at Quinn's ball would not be part of the Coalition. These males would need to speak the human language if they wished to communicate with their future brides.

"Fuck. I will begin mastering their language tomorrow." Tane cursed, and I saw agreement on the faces of the others.

"Might be helpful to be able to speak to the ladies." I tried not to laugh, but being among my brothers again, these free, formidable warlords who would have my back? I hadn't felt so at ease since before my capture.

"Why have you not reported your presence to the Coalition?" Bahre asked. "You wear mating cuffs. You have found your mate. The humans will not be pleased to find one of us living among them in secret."

Buzzkill. Another fantastic human term.

"I needed to find my mate first."

"So you said. You have found her. There is no reason for you to remain on Earth."

If only that were true. "Vivian does not know what I am. She believes I am human."

At that, the corner of Bahre's mouth tipped up and his brows rose in shock and doubt. "There are very few humans as large as an Atlan. And what about when you claimed her? Put your mating cuffs on her wrists? How did you explain the beast fucking her? Claiming her?"

"She has not seen him yet."

"What?" Tane's shocked question was mirrored on all their faces. "What the fuck are you doing? You have not claimed her? You take a great risk. A foolish risk."

"Her brother joined the Coalition and she lost him. She hates the Coalition Fleet, our people, and the war. I could not risk losing her when I was so close to the edge."

"By the gods, you *are* insane." He looked down at my arms, at the mating cuffs clearly visible. "She does not wear the matching pair?"

I shook my head. "Only when we are together. I have convinced her it is part of our sexual play."

"You are in constant pain."

"My beast welcomes the pain. I need it."

Bahre nodded and raised his own arms. "I understand." He looked at Tane and the others. "Come. Let us help our brother hunt the Hive Trackers and save his mate." He looked back to me. "We will need to contact Warden Egara and gather some supplies."

"Will this warden help us?" I asked.

Tane nodded. "She's been here a while and has a mind of her own. She is also human. This will not be her first time breaking Coalition rules."

Human females were indeed fascinating. Every one of them.

Bahre cleared his throat. "We will deal with the Coalition and the multitude of human regulations you have ignored once your mate is safe."

I led the way down, off the rooftop, a group of the most dangerous, deadly fighters in the universe at my back. I'd never been more grateful. For Vivian. For these warlords and their assistance. For the fact that I was alive to claim Vivian. Know her. Touch her. Protect her. Forever.

If she'd have me. The *real* me.

There was a very good chance she would not, especially if staying with me meant being forced to leave Earth and her daughters behind.

ivian, The Fight Club

WAYNE HELD my elbow and *escorted* me inside the parking garage to the cordoned-off area Snook used for his illegal fight club. Which was stupid. We had a perfectly good, *quiet* ambulance parked in the usual space.

"Let me go. This is ridiculous. I agreed to be here, not to sit inside and watch these idiots maul one another."

Wayne shrugged. "Humor me. It's not safe outside. Too much trouble brewing in the neighborhood."

I stopped yanking on my arm and allowed my old friend to walk me to a secluded area nestled between both an exit and two of Snook's fully armed security team. "I'd rather be in the rig."

"Me too, but I got a bad feeling about tonight. Word is there have been some really odd things happening around here in the wee hours. And besides, Snook's less likely to try to hurt your man if you're here to watch." Wayne waited for me to take a seat on a barstool and settled on one next to me.

The barstool wobbled, one leg shorter than the other three, and I wiggled back and forth like a kid as I considered Wayne's words.

I hadn't thought of the benefit of being inside, watching, but Wayne was right. I knew Snook and Maxus—*the Wolf*—had some personal drama. Hell, anyone who worked for Snook had some kind of personal stakes with the man. But I'd known Snook my whole life. He knew I was involved with Maxus, as in sleeping with him. He was a businessman first and always.

Losing me would be bad for business. Losing his Wolf —the best fighter he had—would be bad for business. I didn't trust Snook's personal choices, but I did trust his one true motivation: profit.

"Fine. I'll sit here with you. But anything goes sideways and I'm out of here."

"Sweetheart, I'll lead the way to the door." Wayne grinned at me, took out his pack of cigarettes, realized we were basically inside, and put them back in his pocket with a soft curse.

I laughed softly. "Thank you."

"Turning into a goddamn woman, that's what I'm doing." Gruff words, but he couldn't hide his grin. He leaned back until his shoulders made contact with the cold concrete of the parking garage. I followed his example, the cool, solid wall at my back making me feel better almost immediately.

"So, who's fighting first?" I crossed my arms with a deep sigh.

"New fighters. Both of them. Skinny fuckers."

The first fight was announced, and I had to agree with Wayne. The two fighters were barely more than boys, probably eighteen or nineteen, not fully formed. Too thin. Wiry but strong with a look of desperate hunger and relentless anger in their eyes. I knew the type. They would tear each other to pieces.

No problem. I had plenty of sutures and sterile needle drivers in my bag. Wayne had carried in the medical bag, and it rested at the base of my barstool, ready for action. I had just about everything I might need in that bag. Unless someone required serious attention or a trip to the hospital, I doubted we would need to go outside to the ambulance at all.

My paramedic's uniform was crisp, starched and perfect, just the way I liked it. I had my hair pulled up into a twist to keep it out of my way. I had my oversize purse with me, the bracelets Maxus gave me and the new, sheer black lingerie set I'd ordered online stashed inside, just in case we went to his place after the fights instead of mine. I could not wait to see the expression on my big man's face when I put on all that black and covered myself in flashy jewelry.

I intended to cast a very powerful spell on his cock, one that would keep him hard and eager until morning.

Even better? I'd been especially inspired ahead of our date tonight. I had something special for Maxus to wear as well. As the theme of the night was dark, I also had licorice-flavored body oil to rub all over him as well. Rub on. Lick off.

Bad. So naughty. So much *fun*.

I couldn't stop the smile that crept onto my face. I

loved to play pretend, had since I was a little girl. Becoming a teenage mother and working like a dog notwithstanding, I'd never lost the playfulness I'd been born with. Thank God Maxus seemed to like the playful side of me just fine.

I liked every side of him. The front. The back. The legs. The arms. The face. That sexy, unique hair. I wasn't sure how that mess had ended up on his head, but I would find out eventually. It wasn't normal. He had to have a secret color specialist sworn to secrecy. And if that was the case, I wanted to know who it was because they were brilliant. Talented. And I had been considering adding a few wild streaks to my head as well. Black. Maybe some gold, too. If they could do gold. I figured they must be able to, because some of Maxus's hair was actually silver. Like shiny, metallic, jewelry kind of silver. Some was white. Some black. And there were a dozen shades of gray between.

I rubbed my warm palm against my thigh as the jeering crowd increased the volume. I wanted to rub my hands through his hair, right now. Touch him. Be with him.

Jittery. I was nervous. My hand was shaking. I hadn't even realized it, but I wasn't getting much air into my lungs either and was beginning to feel a bit light-headed. I hated being inside with all these assholes. Their crazed eyes and bulging veins. The bloodier and more vicious the fight, the more these creeps liked it.

And then there were the women with their ruby-red lips and predatory gazes. If Snook ran any kind of prostitution ring, I hadn't seen it. The women here were not being forced, bought and paid for. No, they liked the power their men wielded in the criminal arena. They were trophy wives, some of the bitches equally as cunning and ruthless as their men. Some were worse.

"I hate people." I glanced at Wayne and took a deep breath. "I really do. I hate people. People suck."

He chuckled but didn't take his gaze from the two young men swinging at each other. "You fix 'em up just fine for someone who doesn't care."

"I didn't say I don't care. I said, I hate people." I watched a man raise a glass of whiskey to his lips, swallow the double shot, lift his puffy, pink face to the fighters, and scream at both men, complete with flying spittle and more obscenities than I'd heard since every boy in junior high school thought cursing was the manly thing to do and had diarrhea of the mouth. "Case in point, that one is a real winner."

Wayne followed my gaze. "That's the CEO of StrikeTec United. He's here every week. Drops enough cash on the bookies that Snook would probably fuck the bastard himself to keep him happy."

"Thank you for proving my point." People were generally mean, corrupt, or both. Except my girls.

And Maxus. I'd never met a more honorable man. Everything he did was controlled. Patient. Courteous. He held every door I walked through, held my hand everywhere we went. He helped me cook *and* clean up after. He never allowed me to walk on the outside edge of the sidewalk, and he even insisted on sleeping with his body between mine and the bedroom door.

I had never, ever met anyone like him. It was like he was a fictional character straight off the page of the latest romance novel.

Or an alien.

I chuckled at the thought. He was too good to be the same species as Mr. CEO over there. Or Snook. Or any of the other creeps I'd dated over the years. The girls' rich grandfather and their deadbeat dad sure didn't qualify as honorable, either. Maxus was one of a kind. A miracle.

Shit.

I loved him.

Oh God. No. No. No.

I *loved* him. I was *in love* with him.

This was bad. I did fun and games only and intentionally kept my daughters the top priority in my life. I loved my girls and no one else, not since my mom died. That made every decision simple, every choice easy to make, my priorities in life crystal clear.

I never wanted complicated. And now I had fallen head over heels into *very* complicated.

I didn't know anything about his past. Or his family? What the hell? Why hadn't I asked about his family?

Wait. I had. Whenever I did, he kissed me or touched me or looked at me like I was the most beautiful, amazing woman on the planet and I'd forgotten all about my questions.

Shit. I was weak. Sitting here watching these two young men beat each other to a pulp, I realized that I'd allowed myself to ignore all the warning signs. Why?

Why?

Because I couldn't stop myself from being with him, even if I'd wanted to. Something about him called to me. Moth, meet flame. I'd kept my head in the sand because I honestly didn't want to know if his dad was an alcoholic, or if he had been abused when he was a kid, or if his mother was crazy, or a thousand more difficult and painful scenarios I could list—because I'd seen them all growing up around here. Growing up poor. Vulnerable.

I hadn't wanted to know because if I knew, I would have to make the right choices for my family, to protect my girls and their future, to protect my mental health and hard-won personal boundaries.

If I didn't know how broken Maxus might be, I wouldn't have to act on any knowledge I had about him. I could just play and cuddle and let him have his wonderful, wicked way with me.

Damn it. Now I'd screwed myself over three times as badly. Now I was in love with him. My heart was involved. My soul was involved. My body? Hell, that belonged to him, too. Completely.

"Shit."

Wayne cleared his throat next to me. "Wanna talk about it?"

"No." I didn't want to think about him, either, but now that I'd realized exactly how much trouble I was in, I couldn't *stop* thinking about him. The way he touched me. Kissed me. Held me. Looked at me. God, the way he smelled. His huge...everything.

"Right, then." Wayne grinned at me. He knew. He'd seen Maxus take off with me dangling over his shoulder. "If my opinion is worth anything, I'm happy for you."

"Thanks."

He turned his attention back to the fight, which was nearly over. Red Shorts had Black Shorts down on the ground in a headlock. He would have to tap out soon and pray his opponent was paying attention. Snook paid for a paramedic, but he didn't waste money on a referee.

As if thinking about him too much had conjured him, my cell phone buzzed in my pocket. I pulled it out to find a text from Maxus.

MAXUS - *ARE you at the club?*
   Yes.
   Maxus - Inside?
   Yes. How did you know?
   Maxus – Snook. Stay inside. It's not safe.
   You are being weird. Why?
   Maxus – Do not go outside. We are on our way.

DID HE ANSWER ME? No. No he did not. And we? We? Who the hell was we? And why had Snook suddenly insisted Wayne and I come inside the fighting area where it was hot, smelled like vomit and blood, and I was surrounded by drunk assholes?

I put my phone away and scanned the crowd, paying more attention. Drunks. Rough-looking gamblers here with the rent money. Drug addicts. Men with a bloodlust they could not feed themselves, and women thrilled to be so close to violence. Everything was normal. Wasn't it?

"What's going on? Everything okay?" Wayne asked.

"I don't know. That was Maxus."

"What did he want?"

"He said not to go outside."

Wayne leaned back against the wall, rested his head

on the concrete, and shrugged. "Well then, I guess we don't go outside."

"Something strange is going on."

Wayne's gaze grew dark and serious. "If there's anything outside this club that riles up the Wolf, I don't want a damn thing to do with it. I'm not suicidal. Not tonight, anyway." He chuckled as if he was truly funny, but I was not amused.

And Wayne was not wrong. If Maxus was concerned about my safety, I wasn't going to argue. I had no delusions about my capabilities. I was female. I didn't have a weapon. I wasn't a trained fighter. In this situation I was prey, not predator, and smart enough to accept the truth.

I relaxed back against the concrete, mimicking Wayne's body language, and settled in for a long night. I wasn't leaving this place without Maxus, and that was that. Might as well get comfortable.

The next two fighters were announced, and the betting frenzy began all over again. The two young men who had just beat the living hell out of one another walked side by side to where Wayne and I sat along the wall.

Red Shorts talked first. "You the nurse?"

"I am, indeed. Let me take a look at you." I climbed down off the barstool to inspect the kid. He had a few cuts and scrapes. I cleaned him up and placed butterfly bandages over the worst of his lacerations, then repeated the process with Black Shorts. "How much did Snook pay you gentlemen tonight?" I cleaned out a rather deep wound on the back of Black Shorts' shoulder and had no sympathy when he winced at first contact of the antiseptic. "Was it worth it?"

I always asked. I wasn't sure why, but I felt compelled to know. Usually the fighters would tell me the story of their life. Why they were fighting or for whom. Where they were from. How they'd ended up in this situation.

Red Shorts had just aged out of foster care and was willing to do anything to keep himself off the streets. He had a day job working at a gas station. He had no family.

Black Shorts was fighting to help his mother pay her bills. He had three younger siblings and a father who drank every dollar of his mother's waitressing paycheck.

I'd heard their stories before. More times than I cared to recall.

I slipped them both a business card for a woman I knew who worked for the city. She was in the social work department and helped kids like these find jobs. Real jobs. Not illegal fighting in a parking garage.

They stashed the cards and wandered off. The second fight was going strong, blood already flying. I resumed my position on the barstool and watched the two, slightly larger, slightly older men do battle.

They were circling each other. Taunting.

One stopped dead in his tracks and looked outside of the cage, toward the main entrance. He stood frozen, even as his opponent stepped forward, took a swing, and knocked him on his ass. Out cold.

The victor hopped around, elated, fists raised above his head as he celebrated.

He froze.

Silence moved like slow flowing ice water through the crowd, a wave moving over each person one by one as they became aware of what was happening.

I stood up on the crossbar of the barstool as quietly as

possible and strained to see above the heads of dozens of men far taller than I would have been had my feet been on the ground.

Wayne followed my example, craned his neck.

"Fuck. Get down. Get down now." He grabbed me and pulled me down off my barstool. He reached for my purse and lowered the long strap over my head and shoulder without pause. "Get out of here. Go." He whispered the command, and it sounded like thunder compared to the silence moving through the room.

"*What?*" I mouthed the question, afraid to make the slightest sound.

From the center of the room, a loud, mechanical voice filled the room. "Vivian, mate of Maxus, come forward. If you come to us now, we will spare these people."

Who was that? How did they know my name?

My gaze locked with Wayne's, and I knew mine was filled with glassy-eyed panic. "How do they know my name?" I whispered.

That was enough. The golden man—he looked like a man, kind of, his nose and chin a bit pointy, and the gold paint on his skin didn't help him look *normal*—turned in my direction. His gaze locked onto my position as if he had X-ray vision or something. "Vivian."

His attention caused a second man to move through the crowd toward me.

This man had skin so dark he looked like he was made from the same material as the dark walnut rocking chair my mother had found for me when the twins were born. He literally looked like a moving, living tree. I thought for a split second that he must be from Africa somewhere, straight from an undiscovered tribe with the darkest skin and incredible height, because he was tall. Like, Maxus tall.

Then I saw his eyes.

Copper. Not brown. Not hazel. Copper, like the pipes in a bathroom. He had strange geometric lines drawn all over his face. His nose and chin were pointed, like the golden man's, but as he came closer, I could make out his clothing.

He was covered in some kind of uniform, but nothing like I'd ever seen. Ever. Not even in magazines or on the Internet. The material moved with him, accented every muscle and ligament in his body as if he was encased in shimmering, liquid metal the color of pewter. His muscles were cartoon-level ridiculous. His shoulders? Massive.

He didn't look...human.

I froze like a deer in headlights as the thought moved through me. Not. Human.

"Vivian, mate of Maxus, come with us now." This man's—alien's—voice was not as smooth as the golden one's had been. His words came in stops and starts as if he stuttered or had damaged vocal cords.

Or he was a fucking alien who didn't speak English.

Wayne moved to stand between me and the giant, his presence snapping me out of my paralysis.

"Get away from her and get the hell out of here." He spoke plainly to the alien, his voice steady. I was in awe of his self-control because I shook so badly I doubted I'd be able to speak at all.

The dark giant looked at Wayne and then raised a strange-looking rifle from where he'd had it tucked to his side. He fired.

Wayne's body flew backward, into mine. I wrapped my arms around him, caught him on his way to the ground, and twisted my body in an attempt to keep his head from slamming into the concrete floor.

Kneeling, I checked his eyes. His pulse.

"He's dead." Glancing up at the giant watching me, I was furious now. "He's dead! You killed him!"

"Vivian, mate of Maxus, you will come with us now."

I crawled backward, hoping the extra distance between his towering head and the ground might give me an advantage as I moved toward the exit. "No."

He took another step forward but did not shoot me with his space gun. "Vivian, mate of Maxus, you will come with us now."

"No, I fucking won't," I screamed at him even as the golden one arrived to stand shoulder to shoulder with his friend.

He spoke to me as well, the tone of his voice not quite as deep but equally stilted. "Vivian, you will come with us now."

"No."

Five more feet and I could make a run for it. The parking garage had multiple levels, and this one was nestled half in and half out of the ground. If I could get to the edge, I could jump down, into the palms and lush foliage. There was enough ground cover that I could lose them.

If they didn't have X-ray vision. Or infrared. Or whatever sci-fi shit I couldn't think of at the moment.

I bolted.

Three steps. That's how far I got before golden boy had his hand around my neck and was lifting me off the ground. I grabbed at his wrist, clawing and scratching. He ignored me as if I were no stronger than a newborn kitten. I kicked, my swinging legs completely ineffective.

He carried me, face forward, kicking and clawing, tears streaming down my face, back into the fight club. Back to the copper-eyed demon waiting as if bored.

"We have her. We should transport now."

Golden Boy answered. "He wants Maxus."

"He wants Maxus." The dark one parroted his companion.

They stared at one another for a moment, and a strange buzzing sensation filled the air around me. They seemed to be communicating telepathically or with some kind of transmitter I wasn't familiar with. After a few moments they appeared to reach a decision.

Golden Boy marched back to the center of the club and up to the empty cage. There, he dumped me on the floor, dead center of the fighting area. Without further notice or regard, he stepped out and locked me inside.

All around the club, the humans appeared to be in some kind of haze, hypnotized or something. No one moved. No one cried or screamed or ran for their lives. It was like they were all zombies. Frozen in time like a horror movie come to life.

Who were these guys? And how did they freeze everyone like this? Magic? Alien mind meld, like Spock on steroids? The crowd wasn't talking or moving. They simply watched, every person in the room like a child's doll with empty, glass eyes.

The two aliens stood with their backs to the cage as if guarding me. I could climb the metal fencing, but if I couldn't outrun these things when I was free, there was no way I could get up and over the cage without one or both of them dragging me right back inside.

He wants Maxus.

Who was this *he*? And what did they want with Maxus? Why did aliens—or monsters, or whatever they were—want the man I was in love with?

Surely Maxus wasn't an alien, too. He had a house. A dumpy, seventy-year-old house that needed new paint and new carpet. He had a truck and houseplants and he was wonderful and sexy and everything I'd ever wanted in a man.

He couldn't be an alien. There were no aliens on Earth except the ones they kept locked up behind the walls of the processing centers. The government had made very sure to let every single person know that there were no aliens living among us. Here. On Earth.

They were not welcome. Not wanted. Just...no. He couldn't be.

And if he was? God, they wouldn't let him stay.

I sat and pulled my knees up to my chest. I still had my purse hanging cross-body like a shield. I thought about the lingerie I had inside and nearly began to cry. Wasted now. And the bracelets?

Moving quietly so as not to draw attention, I slipped one hand inside my purse and found the cool metal cuffs he'd put on me that first night. Curling my fingers around the metal, I had to wonder if Maxus had lied to me all this time.

Were these bracelets alien, too? He had made me promise never to put them on unless we were together. Was that because they would do some weird, extraterrestrial voodoo he had been hiding from me?

I studied the mindless bodies that filled the room and bit back a sob. Were they some kind of mind control, too? Were they to make me want him more? Lower inhibitions? Give him anything he wanted? Because I had, and I'd been blissfully happy to do so.

That couldn't be all alien technology and bullshit. I was in love with him.

I. Was. In. Love. With. Him.

Maxus with no last name. Maxus who was bigger than a professional athlete and never talked about his past.

Maxus, the alien.

I lowered my forehead onto my knee, held the bracelet in my hand, and forced my mind to go blank. He would come. I knew that for certain. He would come for me, and these two assholes would wish he hadn't.

 *ivian*

MY POCKET BUZZED.

I froze, peeked up at my two prison guards. They appeared to be engaging in more of their silent buzz talking and paid me no attention.

As discreetly as possible, I pulled my cell phone out of my pocket and onto my lap. My bent knees would hide it from the aliens, and I was more than capable of sending a text with one hand.

My message indicator said I had one text. It was from Maxus.

MAXUS — *I am here.*

. . .

My entire body shivered in relief. Once it started, I couldn't stop shaking.

Maxus - How many are there?
  2 they have guns
  Maxus - Keep your eyes closed.
  ???
  Trust me.

He sent a heart and a smiley face emoji. A goddamn smiley face.

I grinned at my man. I couldn't help myself. Perhaps that had been his intention.

The two aliens abruptly broke off their communication and stood at attention facing the entrance. Both raised their weapons.

I couldn't watch. I'd warned Maxus about the guns. I'd warned him. What else could I do?

Turning my head to the side, I placed my cheek atop my knee and closed my eyes. Then I heard them. Boots. Heavy feet moving together like they were marching. Lots of feet.

What?

The golden one said two words. "Warlords. Seven."

"We knew this could occur. The one called Tane hears us." The dark one seemed to be the stoic grump of the two, although how that was possible, I had no idea. They both seemed more like robots than men. Could one robot be grumpier than another?

"We had no choice." The gold giant spoke as if on the defensive.

"We will not survive." An emotionless statement of fact from the dark alien.

So they were aliens, but didn't they care if they died? Their conversation made no sense to me. None. *Aaaand* I should have kept my mouth shut. I really, really should have—

"You could run away. There is an exit at the back, where you caught me." My eyes flew open, and I attempted to reason with them before I realized what I was doing. They'd killed Wayne in front of me. One shot. Boom. No remorse and no mercy. What was I thinking? They deserved to die.

The dark-skinned alien turned his head slowly as if perturbed that I had dared to speak. "Your mate would hunt us. The outcome would not change."

My mate? I knew he was referring to Maxus, but I wasn't officially his anything. We'd been dating for two whole weeks. Sure, the sex was amazing. He made me laugh and I was totally in love with him—but I didn't have a ring on my finger. As far as I knew, we weren't even exclusive.

Well, I wasn't interested in anyone else, but demanding monogamy wasn't something one usually did after two weeks of casual sex.

Hot, steamy, make-me-claw-the-sheets sex. But still, two weeks was not a marriage or even an engagement. I wasn't even sure if Maxus had ever referred to me as his girlfriend. He liked to talk during sex. He grumbled and said *mine* a lot, but he'd never talked that way when we weren't in the bedroom. Had he? Had I been floating around in a cloud not paying attention?

Sheesh. What a mess.

I lifted my head to watch the entrance for seven what? Warlords?

I had purposely avoided anything and everything about the Coalition Fleet, the Interstellar Brides Program, and the soldiers who went to space to fight. From the moment my brother had opted to leave Earth—and his family—behind, I had refused to learn more. But even I hadn't been able to avoid the insane media frenzy surrounding the *Bachelor Beast* television show. I had not watched a single episode, but I knew that the star of the show, the alien bachelor every available woman on Earth apparently thought was the sexiest creature ever, had been called a warlord. An Atlan warlord. The *Bachelor Beast*.

A beast.

Was this what Maxus was? Was he from the planet Atlan? Was he supposed to be a beast? Some kind of monster? Because Maxus had never, not once, been anything that remotely resembled a beast with me.

Golden One spoke again. "He will kill us if we do not return with Maxus."

"We die a better death here." The dark-skinned alien spoke as if stating a fact, like two plus two is four or the sky is blue, not like he was discussing their impending demise.

The gold creature dipped his chin. "Agreed."

The marching sound drew closer. I scrambled to my feet and moved to the edge of the cage so I could see.

Seven giants walked in formation with Maxus at the

tip of the spear. They were all enormous with wide shoulders and thick chests. Mountains of muscle. Power. Each alien was stunning to look at. Chiseled jaws. Intense eyes. Everything about them, from the way they held their heads to the way they moved their hands, projected confidence. Power. Honor. Control.

Maxus had said he'd fought in a war, that he was a soldier. I had assumed he meant here, on Earth. But as I watched the group of warlords come into the club, I realized that no human army could stand against an enemy force made up of these aliens. Not against the Atlans, and not against my two jailers who were nearly as tall and twice as scary with their oddly colored skin and eyes. Humanity would have zero chance against *either* species. Zero.

The realization was humbling, and I wondered what, exactly, my thick-headed brother had thought he could do out there, in space, with giants like this already fighting?

And why would a man—alien—like Maxus want anything to do with me? Surely their females were amazing creatures. Tall and strong with boobs the size of watermelons? I had curves. I was not thin, not by a long shot, but I was still human.

Why would Maxus want someone like me? Small. Weak. Past my prime breeding years. These aliens wanted to breed with humans, didn't they? Make hybrid alien babies? That was what the conspiracy websites claimed about the Interstellar Brides Program. That alien women were all sterile and they needed to kidnap human woman as breeders.

Hell. They wouldn't have to kidnap anyone, not

looking like they did. But Maxus should be with a twenty-year-old supermodel, not me.

Not. Me.

The warlords' presence disrupted whatever psychic hold my captors had managed to place on the people in the club. All around me people shook their heads to clear them, blinked in confusion, turned this way and that to figure out where they were. They were all acting like they'd been in a deep sleep and woken too early.

One by one, the people froze in awe—or terror—when they recognized the alien standoff happening before them.

Some few, the smart ones, moved toward the exits. Most couldn't seem to gain enough control to think rationally. They stared at me, at the Atlans, at the gold and dark aliens pointing space guns at the warlords. Their mouths opened, closed.

I knew how they felt. I couldn't believe this either.

Maxus led the group of warlords until they stood squarely facing the two bad guys. His gaze landed on me for the smallest moment, and I saw him clench his fists at his sides.

"Release my mate, Prillons. Now."

The golden Prillon seemed to be the designated spokesman for the two. "We are Nexus Six. We require your return to the collective."

Maxus shook his head as if trying to shake a thick, heavy layer of mud from his hair. "Enough."

The one word made every hair on my body raise in alarm. I had never heard that tone from him, that voice.

I stared as his face shifted and his body seemed to expand from the inside, every muscle blowing up like a balloon. His eyes darkened and became harder. Feral. And he grew in height, his entire body rising beyond anything I could have imagined. He had to be eight feet tall.

The beast lifted his cuffed wrists and slammed the metal together, the ringing sound clear as a bell atop a tower.

The beast stood before me. His gaze found me. Locked on.

Hungered.

"Mine."

I'd expected a roar or a growl. The ragged, barely controlled voice shook me to my core. That was not Maxus. Not. Maxus.

The dark Prillon raised his weapon.

Fired.

Chaos. Mayhem.

The other Atlans fought back. Shots were fired. People screamed, running for the exits. The bad guys were making a very loud, horrible buzzing sound like a thousand bumble bees were trapped in the room. Everyone was moving. Screaming.

Maxus leaped over the metal fencing that enclosed the fighting area and landed in a crouch before me.

He rose to his full height.

I stepped back, shocked. Holy shit, he was huge. Angry. Hard as a rock. His cock had grown in proportion to the rest of him. His chest heaved and he stepped forward, towered over me. When I looked up into his eyes, the Maxus I knew was gone. There was only the beast. Need. Hunger. Lust. Glazed, feverish eyes.

"Mine."

$\mathcal{M}$ axus

VIVIAN STUMBLED BACKWARD, trying to get farther from me.

The move infuriated my beast. He was in charge. Totally. Completely. I had waited too long.

"Mine."

Vivian lifted her hands in front of her as if that small action would stop me—him—us. "I heard you the first time, big guy."

I took a step closer. My beast wanted her to run. To fight. To resist. He wanted to punish both of us for making him wait, keeping him locked inside me for so very long.

Years. He'd been locked up for years. If I'd had my way, he would have remained that way until Vivian could accept this side of me—of us.

Maybe forever.

My mate remained remarkably calm. Her back came into contact with the fighting cage, and she stopped moving. "Beast? Um, Maxus? Are you still in there?"

My beast didn't allow me to speak. Instead he leaned down and pressed his nose to our female's neck, breathed her in.

Two small hands pressed against the stretched cotton covering my chest. She was touching us. The beast practically purred with pleasure.

Vivian must have thought the sound was a growl of warning because she pulled her hands back as if burned. "I'm sorry."

"Touch. More." The beast had no fear as he ordered our mate to touch him again.

"Oh, okay. Ummm..." She peeked around us to see what was going on with the two Prillon Hive scumbags who had used her as bait. "Those Prillon thugs are hurting your friends."

To my shock, the beast threw his head back and laughed, the sound like an explosion. I turned my head just enough to assess the situation.

Bahre and Tane had the golden Prillon male tangled up in a specialized net we had acquired, with Warden Egara's help, from the processing center. She had taken us not to the brides' side, but the fighters'. The guards there, friends of Velik's, had provided the magnetized netting and promised that it would prevent a transport beacon from being activated.

They were correct. The golden Prillon, trapped here by the net, fired his rifle at the Atlans repeatedly. He was in a frenzy, desperate to escape, but he was still here. Trapped on Earth with his companion.

The dark-skinned Prillon was one hell of a fucking fighter. He had Kai, Iven, Velik, *and* Egon coming at him. The Prillon was also confined by one of the nets, but he appeared eager to fight, to strike out and inflict pain. Feel pain. Feel anything.

The Hive took everything when they took our minds. Laughter. Fury. Loyalty. Affection. They wiped our minds clean and used our bodies as puppets. This Prillon, it seemed, wanted to feel something. Anything.

As did the beasts who had come with me. They had all transformed into their beastly counterparts. Even Bahre, who had a mate, threw a solid punch at the golden Prillon, hit him in the gut, and grinned.

Both Prillons used their weapons as both rifle and staff, depending on the situation, firing when able, using it to strike when an Atlan got too close.

I'd been confined to my Atlan form when they'd fired their ion rifles at me on that rooftop. My warlord allies had no such limitation. Each shot from the rifles appeared to do nothing more than make them angrier.

These beasts had been away from battle for far too long with nothing to distract them. With the exception of Bahre, they had no mate to protect, to claim and taste and fuck.

No purpose. No home. No foundation.

Vivian. Vivian was my foundation. My home. My purpose.

Mine.

I scanned the area for threats to my female and found none, save one very peculiar female hanging by one hand from a piece of rebar in the ceiling. The loose metal was connected to the parking level above this one. She was holding a camera. Recording this? Taking pictures?

"No!" I bellowed the order at her. Her entire body reacted, jolting as if I'd terrified her. She lowered the camera, and her gaze locked with mine. She was not a threat to my mate, but she needed to get the fuck out of here before Snook or one of the others noticed her presence.

Vivian turned and followed my gaze. Of course she did, my sassy, intelligent female. "Who is that?"

We both watched the woman—she was definitely a human female—pull herself up to the next level of the garage and disappear.

"Gone now." Satisfied that my mate was safe, my beast took one more look around the area.

The humans had run like water flowing out the doors the moment the fighting started. Most of them, anyway. Snook had taken position in a perch above the fray and was watching intently.

I ignored him. He was no threat.

Both Prillon Trackers were down on the ground, held in place by more than one beast.

"Self-destruct."

Were these warlords idiots? Gods be damned, my beast was annoyed.

I—we—he—loomed over Vivian and pointed at the cage floor. "Stay."

"I'm not a dog."

My beast growled a warning, and Vivian promptly plopped down onto her bottom as commanded. My beast growled again for good measure and jumped over the cage once more to land in a crouch on the opposite side. I rose and walked to the dark-skinned Prillon.

"Free or die?" My beast was not into long debates.

The warrior's copper gaze met mine. "Die."

"No!" The golden-skinned Prillon screamed his opposition to this plan. Bahre and Tane held him prone on the concrete, Tane's boot hard pressed to the base of his skull.

Now that both Prillons had been contained, they appeared to have lost the link between their minds. The dark one spoke freely. "He will come for us. He will never stop. We will receive a better death here."

"No." The golden Prillon struggled so fiercely that I moved to Bahre's side and added my foot to the base of the Prillon Tracker's lower back. One hard twist and I would pulverize his spine.

"He will never stop." The dark Prillon looked up at me, met my gaze. "You, Warlord, you know what it is to be hunted by him."

"Yes." My beast knew and was pissed, memories of the time spent in Nexus Six's cage, under his scalpel, fighting for control of my own mind. I knew the power Nexus Six wielded. All too well.

A buzzing filled my head, and I shook myself to be clear of it. To no avail.

"Fuck!" The dark Prillon screamed, and I shared his agony as Nexus Six's presence forced his way into my mind like a mental fist made of splinters and thorns. He tore my mind apart and lodged himself deeply inside my thoughts at the same time.

The Prillon reached for me. *Hear me, Maxus. Kill us. Kill us both.*

Being this close to the warrior, hearing his thoughts,

activated the core communication center implanted deep inside my brain by Nexus Six. It was the way he controlled me, controlled all his *children.* His collective. His Hive.

A crack like thunder exploded inside my skull, and I heard all of them at once. Thousands of voices I had driven from my mind. Ignored. Defeated.

And *him.*

Maxus.

No. I tried to break the connection to Nexus Six. Failed.

I lifted my hands to my head, my beast stumbling backward, away from Bahre and Tane and the Prillon they had captured.

Both Prillon warriors had gone motionless. Silent. Back under their master's firm command. There would be no more pleas from either of them, for life or for death. They were gone now, buried under the weight of Nexus Six and his gathering of minds.

Maxus. I am here.

"No." I spoke aloud, hoping that would help.

Come to me. You are alone.

Cold, stark, agonizing loneliness filled every cell in my body, and my beast bellowed in pain. The agony was not real. The emotion I felt was not real. They were constructs used by Nexus Six to control me. Manipulate me. Use me for his own dark purposes.

I fell to one knee, fighting to get Nexus Six out of my head. I'd done it before. I. Could. Fight. Him.

"Maxus?" I heard Tane's voice as if from a distance, as if he were talking to me from the other end of a long, dark tunnel.

In my mind, Nexus Six made his priorities clear. He pulled my attention to a transport beacon attached to the golden Prillon's uniform. It was there for the taking. All I had to do was take it. I would be with him again. Warm. Part of something bigger than myself. I would *belong*.

My beast's response was a low rumble of pain. I stared at the transport beacon. No matter how hard I tried, I could not look away. My body was no longer my own.

My foot moved. One halting step forward. Nexus Six surged forward in my consciousness, more powerful than he'd ever been before. Omnipresent. He was in my mind. My heart. Every cell of my body his to command.

Kill the others and bring your mate to me, Nexus Six ordered.

Fuck. Fuck. Fuck. No.

"Velik, get the ion blaster. Point it at Maxus," Tane ordered.

"You can't be serious," Velik objected, but he moved quickly to retrieve the blaster rifle and point it at me. "Bahre? Tane?" Velik looked at Tane for clarification. "You sure about this?"

"Can't you hear him?" Tane asked.

"Who?" Velik asked.

"Nexus Six." Tane sounded like he was about to be ill. "He just ordered Maxus to kill all of us and take Vivian to him using that transport beacon."

"Fuck. What a mess." That was Bahre.

I saw all this in my peripheral vision. I didn't care. I was focused on one thing. One. The transport beacon.

I would *not* pick it up.

I would *not* kill these warlords.

Nexus Six was *never* going to get his hands on my female.

Vivian. Gods, Vivian. She was so soft. So curvy. Beautiful. Perfect.

My body moved as if it had a mind of its own, and I jerked closer to the beacon.

"Velik!" Tane barked.

"Fuck." Velik lifted the rifle sight to get a clean shot at me. "Sorry, Maxus. This is going to hurt."

He activated the weapon. Fire screamed through my chest, my left side. No sooner had I felt the blast than Nexus Six shut down the nerves on that side. I was numb. Felt nothing.

I reached for the transport beacon.

Yes! Take it. Bring your mate to me.

 *ivian*

WHAT THE HELL WAS HAPPENING? One minute everything was under control—well, except for the giant beast who sniffed me but barely said two words to me. The next? One of those huge warlords was shooting at Maxus. Shooting. At. Maxus.

I thought they were friends? Or at least on the same side?

The one they'd called Velik fired the Prillon's blaster thing at Maxus. Maxus blinked after the first shot, appeared to be stunned. But then? Velik shot him three more times, and Maxus didn't even change expression. It was like the beast he'd become didn't even feel the blasts.

So what if Maxus had order-growled me to stay here, out of the way? If I gave him the benefit of the doubt, which I realized I actually had, I assumed it was to keep me safely out of the way.

But what now? His own beast friends were turning on him? And he was acting strangely.

I had to get the hell out of here and let them sort this all out. But how?

Frantic for an escape route that would keep me as far away from *all the aliens* as possible, I looked everywhere. I saw Snook hiding in one of his specially built balconies. He wasn't watching me; he was watching events unfold with calculation in his eyes. Bastard. He was probably trying to figure out how to get his hands on those alien weapons so he could sell them on the black market. Ever the entrepreneur.

My gaze roamed farther, and I saw the same woman I'd seen earlier, the photographer, had returned. Or rather, she'd probably never left, just changed position, worked her way around the edges of the ceiling to a new vantage point.

Crazy. She had to be fucking insane. No picture was worth this.

She was pretty, not much older than my daughters, and appeared calm and collected, as if she did this kind of thing every day. She was barely visible through a crack in the concrete near an older elevator shaft. The elevator had moved people between floors of the parking garage back in the day. Before Snook had bought the place. The elevators still worked, but only if you had a special key. Very few people had one, and I was not counted among them.

The woman moved her camera to the side so she

could make eye contact with me and pointed to the corner farthest from the fighting cage.

Of course she would suggest *that* exit. But she had a point. If I could get out of the cage, I could move around the outside edge of the fighting area, keeping the cage between me and all the warlords. That exit was also in the darkest part of the club, *and* closest to a network of alleys I'd been running in my whole life. I could disappear in a matter of seconds out there in my neighborhood. This was my home turf. I knew every route and every hiding place nearby.

But heaven help me if I had to run very far. I was not sixteen anymore. I was twenty years older, much heavier, and not nearly as active. If I had to sprint, I probably wouldn't make it more than a block, maybe two. That was if I were willing to ignore the stitch in my side and vomit on the way.

Didn't matter. I had to make a run for it before all these aliens remembered I was here.

I nodded at the photographer. She withdrew with a small salute. I didn't know if she was going to try to meet me outside or if she was wishing me luck. Probably the latter. I doubted these Atlan warlords wanted their pictures taken. And I really, really didn't think the Feds would want the public to see the Prillon guys attacking and killing humans in a Miami fight club. If she had taken pictures of those Prillons, there would be no mistaking them for human. The darker alien might pass for a human. From a distance. If no one saw his eyes. But the walking metal statue with golden eyes? No chance at all.

I twisted my head to look for Wayne and regretted the

decision instantly. Wayne's body hadn't moved. He was still dead, slumped at the base of a barstool, skin ashen and eyes wide open with shock. At the sight, all I wanted to do was crawl to Maxus and ask him to wrap those giant arms around me and keep me safe. Hold me. Lie to me and tell me everything was okay.

None of this was okay. Not even fucking close to okay.

"Damn it." I was getting out of here. Now.

I moved slowly but quickly. All the warlords seemed to be completely focused on Maxus. He was kneeling by the golden Prillon, the one in the net. Maxus held his head in his hands, and he looked like he was in horrible pain. Terrible. Agonizing. I'd never seen lines that deep around his eyes and mouth. I triaged trauma patients. Car accidents. Burn victims. I knew pain when I saw it.

Maxus wasn't just in pain; he was drowning in agony.

The urge to go to him was so strong that I opened the cage door and took a step toward him before I realized what I was doing. A deep growling sound erupted from his throat, and he began rocking back and forth as if he were being tortured somehow, from the inside.

That beast was not Maxus. I needed to remember that. *That* was a beast—whatever that meant. I knew they were the most feared fighters in the Coalition. I knew that if they didn't find a mate, they died from some kind of fever. And thank you *Bachelor Beast* advertising campaigns for that very valuable—*completely useless* —information.

All I knew for sure was that Maxus's beast had looked at me like he was going to devour me alive, and there hadn't been even the smallest trace of the man I loved in its eyes. No possessive grin. No tenderness. No desire or passion or coherent thought at all. It was like he was a wild animal, all instinct and no control. Like a rabid dog who happened to be strong enough to literally tear me in half.

Was Maxus's behavior caused by the strange fever the television ads had been talking about? The show had made a very big, *huge* deal about how the warlord would be executed if he got the fever. That if they lost control of their beast, there was nothing anyone could do.

I stared at Maxus as he rocked back and forth. I tried to breathe around the massive cavern of pain crushing my heart. Were my ribs collapsing, forming a crater inside my chest? Putting pressure on my lungs and heart, making it impossible to move.

Maxus. God. He had the fever. He had lost control of his beast. He was in pain. Disoriented. Confused. He had the fever, and now his friends were going to kill him.

A sob escaped and I stepped backward, fighting to keep my balance. I wrapped the fingers of one hand around the metal links of the cage to orient myself as I mentally worked up the courage to turn and run.

I couldn't watch him die. God couldn't be this cruel. He just couldn't. I'd finally given my heart away and now...

Turning away, I took one step. Two.

Stopped with another sob. Shaking. My knees struggled to support my weight. My feet refused to move.

I couldn't do this. I couldn't leave him. Not like this. They were going to *kill* him.

Maybe, just maybe, I could get my hands on one of those Prillon space guns. If I hurried around the outside edge, I could grab the weapon before the others realized what I was doing. Maybe, I could get them to stop hurting Maxus. Then again, I was an idiot. There were six massive aliens—not including the asshole Prillons who had murdered Wayne—in this room.

Maxus roared and slammed his closed fists on the ground.

He was a mess. If there was even the smallest chance I could save him, I had to try.

"This is insane. I'm insane." Talking to myself now, too? Well, at least I was correct. What I was about to do was irrational.

Maybe I was foolish. What I did know, was that I was in love. With that lying, secret keeping alien they were about to murder in front of me.

I made my move, stumbled around the outside edge of the fighting cage as if I were making a run toward the corner exit I had chosen. When I reached the place closest to the Prillon weapon on the ground, I kept my gaze focused on my goal and ran toward it.

Three steps and ran into a hard wall of pure muscle.

"What are you doing?" The warlord, the beast called Tane, stood in front of me, blocking my path.

"I can't watch you kill him." I hoped Tane would assume I was trying to run. I didn't say I was going to grab that weapon, point it at every single alien in the room except *mine,* and hope like hell I could figure out how to shoot.

Tane growled. He was massive, like the others. I knew this was his beast, the big, bad part of him that the entire universe seemed to be afraid of. But his eyes were clear. I could see a man—alien, whatever, a *person*, behind the eight-foot giant's eyes. A sane, rational, thinking being.

"You don't scare me, Warlord. Get out of my way."

Tane took a deep breath and closed his eyes. After a few seconds, his body began to change, becoming smaller, his face more refined, his jaw less pronounced. His massive shoulders changed from giant sized back to massive-for-a-human size. A very tall human. He was a man—male—again.

"I will not allow you to leave him, not like this." His voice had become more succinct, and he was speaking in full sentences again. Great. It changed nothing. I was not going to watch them kill Maxus. I couldn't do it.

"I'm not leaving him. You're the ones killing him."

"We are trying to save him."

"Bullshit." At that exact moment, Velik fired at Maxus again and his beast groaned at the blast. Suffering. "You guys are hurting him."

"This is your fault, female. Why are you not helping him?" Tane scolded me like I was a child, his dinner-plate-sized hand wrapped gently, but firmly around my upper arm and shoulder. He glanced down at my hands, or at least, I thought he was looking at my hands. "Where are your mating cuffs? You are his mate. He should not be like this. If you don't help him, he *will* die."

"My fault? *My fault?* What the hell are you talking about? How does this have anything to do with me?" Tears of frustration, anger, confusion, pain, loss—my emotions were a jumble, and they were all about Maxus. "You're the ones shooting him, killing him. Not me."

"Fuck. He really didn't tell you anything, did he?" All the anger and outrage seemed to drain out of Tane's body with his words.

"What was he supposed to tell me? That he was an

alien? That he got infected with an alien fever that is killing him? That some even scarier aliens called Prillons were going to show up and kill my friend right in front of me? Try to kidnap me? What, exactly, was he supposed to tell me?"

Tane's gaze softened, and I realized he was gorgeous in his own way. He wasn't Maxus, but he was a truly beautiful man. Alien. Shit. He was an alien. *Remember that.*

"He was supposed to tell you that you are his mate. That from the moment he met you, he would live and die to protect you. Fight for you. Kill for you. Do everything in his power to ensure your happiness, your comfort, and your pleasure."

That last made my cheeks flush with heat. Oh, he'd done a very good job of—

"He was supposed to explain to you that, as his mate, you are the only one who can save him from the affliction we call mating fever."

"If it's only about—you know—mating, we've had sex lots of times and—" I dipped my head toward where Maxus and the others seemed to be frozen in some kind of standoff. "Apparently, sleeping with me didn't do the trick. So, I don't know what you expect me to do. I can't help him."

Tane blinked slowly. A flush filled his cheeks, and he chewed at his bottom lip for a split second before clearing his throat. Was he embarrassed?

"Did you have sex with his beast?"

"Did I—" *What?* I knew my eyes must look like they were about to explode out of the sockets, but I couldn't even wrap my head around the question. "What? No. I didn't even know he was—I thought he was human."

"Fuck." Tane's eyes narrowed as if he were in pain. "Did he at least give you the mating cuffs? He wears the matching pair and is using the pain to help control his beast. So, you must have worn them, at least once, when you—you know?" He *was* blushing. Somehow, that made this alien a lot less threatening and more adorable. Maxus was sexy as hell. But this one?

I stared at Tane, waiting for him to finish. His cheeks darkened from pink to red.

"Had sex?"

"Yes. Thank you. When you...had sex."

"Yes, I wear them when we are together."

He sighed in relief. Yes, he was adorable. Like a lost puppy. He looked a lot younger than Maxus, too. If he wasn't an alien, I might try to set him up on a blind date with one of my daughters. But he *was* an alien. And my daughters weren't going to outer space. Neither was I. I didn't care how great the sex was. Home was home and outer space was—well, terrifying. Outer space was the monster that had swallowed up my brother and killed him. The place where those Prillon bastards came from, the ones who murdered innocent people without batting an eye.

"Where are they now?" He used the hand on my arm to nudge me in the direction he wished me to go. Toward Maxus. Back into the mess.

Velik fired a blaster shot right into Maxus's chest as we approached. I gritted my teeth to keep myself form either screaming at Velik or walking up to him and slapping him. Maxus was on his knees already, but he doubled over when the blast hit him, his forehead nearly touching the concrete. Immediately, he rose once more, his gaze locked onto something that looked like a big button lying forgotten on the concrete. He didn't look away from the button. Didn't blink. But he didn't reach for it either.

What was he doing? His eyes were blank and empty. It was like he wasn't even in there, like his body was just a shell being directed by some asshole teenager with a remote control.

"Maxus." His name was more a prayer than anything. He was so zoned out I didn't expect a response. I didn't even think he would hear me.

He roared in agony and fell to the ground, rolling with his hands on his head as if he were fighting himself. Rolling *away* from the button. *Away from me.*

Velik looked at me, then Tane. "Whatever you are going to do, do it fast. He won't last much longer."

13

"DOES SHE HAVE THE MATING CUFFS?" Another warlord had returned to normal—also known as *'still huge'* size—and I noticed that he wore cuffs around his wrists. They were about the same size, as well as the same color, as the cuffs Maxus wore, but that's where the similarities ended.

This man's—alien's—'mating cuffs' were beautiful. The metal Maxus wore was plain. Smooth. As were the bracelets—mating cuffs—he had given me. The cuffs this Atlan wore were decorated with ornate, delicate designs. Beautiful geometries offset with hues of silver, pewter, and gold. The lines carved into the cuffs looked like they were moving and blending into one form, yet I could not determine where one design began and another ended.

"Maxus didn't give me anything that looked like that."

Velik cleared his throat. "I had to buy his mating cuffs

on the black market. Sneak them to Earth inside a transport of supplies from Atlan. His cuffs are without familial markings. My apologies, my lady. I did not know which family lineage Maxus is from. He did not provide the information, and I did not ask. Therefore, your mating cuffs are not what a lady might desire."

"Warden Egara is going to kick your ass," Tane said. Velik looked disturbed by the thought but returned his attention to me at once.

"It's fine." I didn't give two shits whether or not the metal bracelets Maxus had given me were fancy or plain. Did. Not. Care. I was not really a jewelry person anyway. Never had been. Wearing a big, expensive piece was just asking to have your house robbed, your person mugged, or worse.

"Then, you do have them?" The mated warlord asked.

"Who are you?" I wasn't telling him anything until I knew who he was. Maybe that was stubborn, but I felt like I was a leaf in the wind already. Information was power, right? At the moment, I felt like I had none of either.

"I am Bahre, my lady. Mate of Quinn. This is Tane, Velik, Kai, Iven, and Egon. We are from Atlan." He indicated each of the large aliens in turn. Kai, Iven, and Egon were busy dragging the Prillons to the side, away from Maxus. The Prillons were quickly restrained, and the Atlans placed a gag of some sort over them, covering their mouths. Which was just fine with me. I didn't want to hear anything either one of them had to say. Murderers.

Wayne killers.

"My lady, Vivian, please. Do you have the mating cuffs?" Bahre asked.

How did he know my name? Stupid question. He'd come here with Maxus to fight these Prillon guys. Maxus must have told all of them about me.

"Yes. I have them." I patted my nearly forgotten sling purse with my hand. "But he didn't tell me what they were for."

Bahre moved to stand before me, then knelt on one knee like he paid homage to a queen.

"My lady, you must put the mating cuffs on and claim Maxus...and his beast. You must deem him worthy and accept the beast into your body. Only then will his beast be completely under your control."

"Under my control? Are you crazy? That makes zero sense."

Tane touched my shoulder, gently, as if afraid I would bolt. "Once our beast feels the instinct to claim a mate, he grows stronger. Wilder. Every male is a threat, friend or foe. Every female who is not his mate is seen as a deceiver, a trickster, an obstacle between the beast and his true mate. Only the beast can choose. And once he has chosen, he will accept no other. Listen to no other. When the mating fever takes over, the beast loses himself, his pain so great that he can do nothing but destroy. Kill. Even those he once cared about. He is lost."

"And that's why you execute them?"

No one answered my question. They didn't need to.

A lump the size of an orange settled in my throat. I couldn't talk. Couldn't think. Pain spread from my throat to the rest of me, my blood like gasoline fueling the pain-fire. Hot tears streaked my cheeks, so bitter and angry they burned my skin as they passed, their taste acid on my tongue when I licked them from my lips.

Maxus moaned, his back arching up off the ground as if he were being electrocuted. Tortured. Nothing made sense. What was happening to him? Was this suffering the effects of the fever? "Are you telling me that Maxus is like that because of mating fever?"

Tane's voice was hollow. Bereft. "No, my lady. The Nexus unit who captured him reactivated a connection to Maxus's mind. He is fighting Maxus for control, causing him great pain. Maxus does not have a mate to ground his beast, so he is fighting the beast as well."

Oh God. "What does the Nexus thing want?"

"He wants Maxus to kill all of us, take you, and use the transport beacon on the floor to return, with you, to the Hive."

"Take me?" I looked anew at the strange button lying on the ground. "Is that it? The transport thing?"

"Yes."

"Why don't you just get rid of it?"

"If we go near, Maxus attacks," Velik supplied, firing another shot at Maxus, this time hitting his hand, the hand reaching toward the transport beacon.

Maxus roared in fury before his body contorted, jerking movements taking him farther from the button. Now that I understood, I could see the battle going on. Maxus fighting his beast. His beast fighting the Nexus mind control. The Nexus—whatever the hell that was—fighting to control them both.

I'd never been so terrified in my life.

"How am I supposed to get him to listen to me? I don't know what to do."

Bahre lifted his bowed head and looked at me, eye-to-eye, despite the fact that I stood straight and he was on one knee. "Once a beast has chosen, he will obey and serve only one person in the universe."

"His mate?"

"His mate." Bahre turned his head to where Maxus continued to writhe in agony. "Maxus is fighting the fever, the rage of his beast. He is also battling the Hive collective that captured him and took over his mind. He broke their hold once, to come here, to find you. He fought—and won—for you, for the hope that he might find you."

The thought humbled me. I was no one. Nothing. But these Atlans were telling me that out of all the women, alien and human, in the entire freaking universe, Maxus's beast had chosen me. Would obey me. Serve me. Protect, love, adore, worship...*me*.

"But I'm nobody. Seriously. Why me?"

"The beast has chosen. You are his and he is yours."

The words were so close to something Maxus had said to me that my entire body shivered in recognition. "Okay. I'm his mate. He's mine. Only I can save him. I get it. But what am I supposed to *do*?" I motioned to where Maxus continued his mental and physical battle. "He's totally out of control. I'm not that strong. There is no way I can get close to him if he's like this."

Bahre's gaze turned cold. "What are you willing to sacrifice to save him?"

The question hit me like a punch to the gut. The answer shocked me, but I knew what I would say the moment he asked.

"Anything."

My girls were adults. I'd taken care of them, raised them, sacrificed everything to give them the best I could. And I was tired. So goddamned exhausted. Tired of working two jobs. Tired of being mother and father to my kids. Seriously, would it kill the girls to have to take their laundry to a laundromat instead of bringing it home every week? Surely not. I didn't want to do this anymore. I was sick and tired of taking care of everyone else in the world but myself.

Maxus was mine. I was his. We both deserved some happiness. Someone to depend on. Someone to take care of who would take care of us in return. And yes, I wouldn't turn down a few more orgasms, either.

Me and Maxus? We deserved our fucking happily-ever-after. Now that this Nexus thing was trying to take that away, I was beyond furious.

Maybe outer space wouldn't be that scary if I were with him. And if I could visit Adrian and Stefani a few times a year. With those transport things, surely, that wouldn't be an issue. Right?

Bahre had remained silent as I processed my thoughts. I focused to find him staring at me. Waiting.

"Are you willing to die for him?"

"What?" When had death become an option?

"We cannot allow you near him unless you know and accept the risk."

"What risk? I'm his mate, right? He is supposed to obey me?" The room spun. Was I still breathing? Yes. Standing? I searched for my feet. They were glued in place, cold as lead bolts securing me to the floor.

"Normally, yes. There is nothing normal about this situation. If we sedate him, bring him awake slowly, there is a chance he will not be able to regain control of his mind. The Hive intruder may force him to do things he does not wish to do. With his pain, his beast may be too far gone to recognize his mate and may see only an enemy when you approach. If that is the case, he will attack. He could kill you. Please understand. Maxus would not want you to come to harm. He would rather die than see you hurt." Bahre had lowered his voice, speaking quietly, only to me. "We will not judge you harshly should you wish to leave now. Nor would Maxus blame you, my lady. His first and only concern is your safety and happiness."

"If I leave, you're going to kill him, aren't you?"

"We would be honoring his final wish in doing so."

"What final wish is that?"

"To protect you."

The air left my body in a whoosh, and I nearly collapsed. Tane caught me from behind and held me upright as tears streamed, unchecked, down my face. He was right, this Atlan. I closed my eyes, and all I could see was Maxus staring at me like I was his sun and moon. I could feel my mate's hands on me, worshipping me with every touch. He'd done nothing but love me from the moment we met, and I'd been blind, thinking he was human. Doubting him and his intentions. I hadn't loved him back enough. I'd taken and taken and taken every-thing he gave me and demanded more. I. Took. *Everything*.

"Maxus." Oh, God. This was not happening.

I stared into the alien's eyes and knew he meant what he said. Every word. If I wasn't willing to risk my life, to die for my mate, they would kill Maxus, honor him and his final wish. Honor his mate. Me. They would kill their friend, no matter how much it hurt them to do so, because it was the right thing to do.

"Tell me what to do."

Bahre stood slowly and looked over my shoulder at Tane. "Let's do this."

Tane squeezed my arm gently before moving around me. He withdrew a small device from his pocket, held it for a moment, then raised his head to look at the others. "We're only going to get one shot at this."

"Tell me when. I'll hit him a couple times to keep him down." Velik repositioned the blaster rifle tightly into his shoulder and stared down the sights. "Any time."

Tane waited for Kai, Iven, and the others to nod. All the warlords, including Bahre, moved slowly in a circle around Maxus as Velik kept his weapon ready to fire.

I thought Maxus oblivious until he rolled onto his hands and knees, fought to pull one leg up so he was kneeling, ready to rise. "Stay back!" His beast roared the order, but the Atlans ignored him.

"Now!" Tane yelled.

Velik fired not two, but three hard, fast blasts into Maxus's body. If a beast could scream, I would say that's the sound that came out of my mate. There was so much pain in his voice that I doubled over like they'd shot me instead. The tears hadn't stopped. I wrapped my arms around my waist and shook all over as the others leaped on top of Maxus, each Atlan insanely strong and brutally efficient. Merciless. Bahre grabbed my mate's head and shoved his cheek to the ground so hard I was afraid he would crack Maxus's skull.

"Hold him!" Tane rolled his body on top of Maxus's hips as each of the others held down an arm or leg.

Five beasts, and still Maxus moved them. All of them.

His bellows of rage accompanied a shift in the pile of Atlan bodies, rising and falling like ocean waves.

Holy shit.

"Fuck, he's strong," Kai grumbled.

"Hurry the fuck up, Tane." Bahre, who was holding Maxus's head while trying to avoid his teeth, struggled to maintain his grip.

"Fuck." Tane placed the device he held against the back of Maxus's thigh and activated something.

I heard a strange hissing sound coming from the device. Tane cursed as Maxus rolled his body, moved his thigh, tried to escape whatever was happening there. Tane moved with him, holding on for dear life even when his head slammed into the concrete.

"How long?" Velik asked.

"The doc said a minute, maybe two, depending on the number of integrations."

"Why don't we let him go?" Kai spoke through gritted teeth, and I saw that Maxus had his hand wrapped around Kai's throat. "Wait it out." Kai grabbed Maxus's hand and tried in vain, to remove my mate's death grip. Kai pulled on Maxus's hand, and I heard bones cracking like dry twigs.

Whose bones? Kai's? Or had he just broken the bones in my Maxus's hand?

"He could kill one of us if he had two minutes," Bahre pointed out.

"Fuck. Didn't the doc have anything stronger?" Iven asked.

"Only if we were willing to risk killing him," Tane informed him.

I stood helpless, arms wrapped around my middle

and my mind spinning as everything in my life spun on its axis.

I was in love with an alien.

I had agreed to try to save his life. I wasn't sure exactly what that might entail, but I had a feeling—based on Tane's embarrassed hue a few moments ago—that having sex with the beast was going to be involved. Not Maxus. The beast. The bigger, stronger, out-of-control beast that five warlords could barely contain.

Part of me wanted to run screaming from the place and never look back. But there was another part of me, a hungry, lustful, desperate side that wanted that beast to shove his cock inside me and fuck me until I couldn't think straight. That wanted him a bit out of control. Wild. For me. Only for me.

I knew Maxus was in love with me. What would it be like to be loved by the beast part of him as well?

A minute passed. Two. I knew because I checked the fight clock on the wall. It was still running, forgotten in the chaos of the last few minutes, ticking the seconds that felt like hours.

Maxus did not relent.

They held him down. Cursed. More bones cracked.

I shuddered. Waited. When I couldn't stand it another moment, I walked toward Maxus, got down on my hands and knees, and crawled toward his head.

"Stay back, female," Velik ordered.

"Shut up. You do you. He's my mate."

I heard Velik scoff like I was an idiot, but I glanced at Bahre's face and I saw respect there.

"You are a worthy female. Maxus has chosen well."

"I hope so." I laid down as close as I dared, face-to-face with Maxus's beast, and prayed for it to be over.

When Maxus finally stopped moving, he collapsed like a dead man, unaware and utterly still on the cold concrete floor. I collapsed, too. And cried.

14

M *axus, Interstellar Brides Processing Center, 24 hours later...*

ONE MINUTE I was writhing on the floor trying not to reach for the transport beacon, fighting Nexus Six for control of my beast. Every thought and particle of will in my body had been focused on resisting his order to betray my mate. The next, a sharp pain spiked in my thigh. Warmth spread through me. Heat. Time seemed to slow down. The other warlords became fuzzy outlines.

They had attacked. Restrained me.

My beast had lost control, gone berserk. Convinced the other warlords were trying to kill me. I'd fought with every ounce of strength I possessed. Bones had cracked, the pain nothing compared to the agony of what felt like acid pouring into my skull from my integrations.

Nexus Six had forced his own psychic strength into me; the integrations that lined the inside of my skull had buzzed to life like a thousand honeybees inside my skull. My beast had fought with everything he had, all his strength. All his will.

Still, I'd been defeated.

Vivian.

Gods, Vivian's tear streaked face had been so close. So close to mine. Watching me die. Suffer. Fail her as both her protector and her mate.

Had I hurt her? Killed her? Where were the other warlords? Had I betrayed them all? Killed them? Was Nexus Six torturing Vivian at this very moment? Why could I not remember what had happened to me? To her?

My mate.

A growl drifted from my throat, and I realized my body was in beast form. I had not shifted back when I'd lost consciousness. I could not see. Everything was black.

Neither my form nor my blindness were good signs. It was too late. I'd lost Vivian. The pain in my wrists and arms was gone. The mating cuffs must have been removed as they no longer anchored me, triggered my pain response, reminded me to think of her. Streaks like fire should be rushing up my forearms to my shoulders, each jolt a reminder to my beast that I had a mate waiting for me. A welcome and much needed reminder to remain in complete control. For her. Only for her.

Now there was nothing. I was lost.

I focused on listening. Heard nothing. Silence. There was nothing in my mind but quiet. No Hive buzzing, no Nexus Six. Nothing.

Why was I conscious? Thinking? They should have killed me. I'd discussed this with the Warlords Bahre and Tane before we entered Snook's club. They had their orders. The moment Nexus Six had made his play, they should have killed me. Fucking bastards. Gods be damned, those fucking—

"Maxus? Can you hear me?"

My pillow moved. No, not a pillow. Vivian?

I turned my neck slightly and realized my head rested on something warm and soft. A steady, calming heartbeat was pressed to my right ear. The scourge of Nexus Six was gone from my mind, and in his place...her.

I could smell her now, the heady sweetness of her skin, unique and only hers. My head was in Vivian's lap. Something moved over my forehead. Through my hair. She was...touching me.

My beast stiffened in complete shock, assessing the situation. Was she in danger? Where were we?

I tried to open my eyes, to find her. My body was paralyzed; my eyelids refused to obey.

I could not move.

Fighting to be free of whatever curse had taken hold, my body began to tremble. Shake. I had to break free. Protect Vivian. Fight.

"Maxus, it's okay. Everything is okay. We're safe. Come back to me." Gentle fingers moved over my forehead and cheeks. Stroking me. Petting me. I struggled to clear the remaining chemical fog from my mind. As I did so, my beast responded to our female. My cock hardened, rising to our mate's siren call. Her fascinating scent surrounded me. Hypnotized me.

Made me *want*.

"Mine."

Vivian's body stilled, her hand no longer stroking my cheek, simply resting against my skin. Seconds later, her soft laugh moved through me like a warm wave. "So you are awake, my beast. Come back to me, Maxus. Open your eyes and pretty please...don't be crazy."

Come back? As in return to her? I had never left her. Never would. Not while I lived and breathed. She was mine. I was hers. Without her, I was nothing. Dead.

My beast agreed. As he was the one currently in control, I had no choice but to wait and discover what he would do next.

My mate shifted, her body pressed to the right side of my face as she wrapped herself around my head. Her left arm pulled me closer to her breasts. Her right rested on my chest, the slight weight somehow more powerful at keeping me in place than all five of the Atlan warlords had been when piled on top of me, fighting me. I would not move from beneath her touch. Not willingly. My beast had never felt such peace.

But then, I'd never allowed him access to our mate, too afraid that she would reject us. Condemn us. I had not had the courage to reveal my true nature to her. My beast—and I—had suffered greatly for that choice. I could not bring myself to regret it.

"Maxus?"

"Vivian." My beast spoke her name, the deep rumble filled with satisfaction neither one of us had any interest in hiding from her.

"Are you in control? Bahre said you might go crazy and try to kill me."

"Never hurt. Mine."

Her body shuddered around me as if the words caused a staggering amount of relief to our female.

"Where?" As usual, my beast had little interest in utilizing our full vocabulary.

"We are in a containment cell beneath the Interstellar Brides Processing Center in case you go crazy. Velik arranged it with a really nice woman, Warden Egara? Do you know her?"

"No." I turned my neck so that my face pressed more firmly into Vivian's body. I could not get close enough. "Mate."

"Yes, beast. It's nice to meet you."

"Sorry. Lied."

Vivian sighed and the sad sound made my beast want to rip something in half, mainly himself—me. "I understand. I wish you would have told me, but I understand why you didn't."

"Can't stay. Earth. Go home."

"I know. You have to go to The Colony or back to Atlan. Bahre and Tane explained everything to me. And someone named Dr. Surnen wants to see if he can figure out your Hive integrations because he said it could help other Atlans with mating fever to control their beasts. Maybe survive long enough to find a mate."

"Go home. With mate." She understood so much now, but not the most important thing. That I could not be without her. Would not survive a lengthy separation. That she was my anchor, my life, the only being I cared about. She was everything. "Mine."

"I know that, too." She began to cry, and I could smell her tears, the hint of salt in the air making my beast crazed. I needed to touch her, but her words froze me in place.

"I made my choice, Maxus. When you were lying there, dying, I made my choice. I chose you. I'll go with you to Atlan or The Colony. I don't care where we go. I'm yours and you're mine. I have the mating cuffs on. I'll be your mate."

"Girls." I had to know she had thought this through. She would never leave her daughters, and I would not ask her to.

"They can visit, right? Or we can visit them? They're grown adults. I raised them. I gave them everything for a long, long time. I want something for myself now. This is crazy, and I've only known you a few weeks, but...I love you. I want to go with you. Be with you. I need you, Maxus." She leaned over, pressing herself to me with as much strength as she could muster. "I don't want to lose you. I love you. I love you. I love—"

Desire flooded my body. Relief. Lust. Need.

Love. Fuck me, I loved this female to distraction. I didn't understand what that would mean before I'd found her. Now I knew the truth. I would kill for her, die for her, sacrifice anything and anyone to make her happy. She. Was. Mine.

My beast made a sound I'd never heard before, the emotion behind it ripped from my soul and given to her, Vivian, our mate.

At one with my beast and free to move at last, I shook off the last, lingering effects of the injection the others had given me and rolled over, coming up on my knees. I lifted my head to find Vivian seated with her back leaning against the wall. Beneath us both was a large mattress covered with clean, serviceable bedding. Nothing fancy or colorful, the fabric was a dull gray with burgundy icons scattered across the entire surface, the symbols for the Coalition Fleet. The symbol I had fought for, nearly died for.

The symbol that had led me off my home world of Atlan, to her.

The mattress was settled on the floor of a room large enough to hold several prisoners. An energy field made up the entire front wall. I knew from experience, there would be no breaking through that force field. The lighting was dim, as if the softer illumination would be less upsetting once my beast realized we were in a prison cell.

I had the last laugh. My beast didn't fucking care right now, not when we had Vivian with us, wearing my mating cuffs around her wrists and...*that.*

I reached for her, my beast nearly purring when she did not pull away from his touch. My fingertips came into contact with the most delicate, sheer fabric I had ever seen in my life. I could see through the sheer black material every bit of Vivian's skin, every curve visible beneath the garment. The fabric hugged her curves, a kind of bodysuit that placed her breasts on prominent display. The lines of the tight garment followed the curves of her waist and hips, disappearing at the vee between her legs as if pointing me in the direction she wished me to go.

"What is this?" I wanted to both caress her through the fabric and tear it from her body.

"Do you like it?" She ran her hands over the tops of her thighs where my large head had left marks in her sensitive skin. "It's called a catsuit." She pointed to the nearest corner where I saw her large purse had been left in a heap on the floor. "I had it with me when...you know. It was part of the surprise."

"What else?" Fuck, this female was fascinating, and my beast wanted to play even more than I had.

"You like it?"

"Yes."

She scrambled away from me and off the bed to her bag, where she reached inside and began pulling additional items from the mysterious depths. "This goes with it. And these. Oh, and this..."

"Show me." My beast remained unmoving, literally incapable of breaking the spell our mate was weaving around us. I wanted to know what her strange items were meant to do, and I enjoyed the anticipation of that discovery nearly as much as I knew I would enjoy fucking her in the sexy outfit.

When she was finished pulling items from her bag, she walked back to the bed and placed them on the bed. With a smile I was addicted to, she reached for the first item and put it on. It was a black silk mask with holes for her eyes. Next was a pair of black gloves that covered her to her wrists. She pulled them over the mating cuffs, but I told the beast to take his protest and shove it up his ass. The cuffs were there. The rest was for...fun. Seduction. Play.

The gloves were followed by a collection of sparkling jewelry that shone like the brightest diamonds around her throat, a large, central pendant hanging from the center to dangle between her breasts. She clasped more jewelry around her wrists, in her hair, placed pieces dangling from each ear until she looked like a sparkling gift I could not wait to unwrap.

Last, she lifted an arced piece to her head and secured

it in place. When she lowered her hands, I saw that the item created the illusion of pointed black ears.

She put her hands on her hips and tilted one hip toward me. "Meow. This is my naughty kitty outfit."

The rumble coming from me was more like a running engine now. My beast rose from his position on the bed and walked toward our mate. The clothing I still wore, I ripped from the beast's body as I neared her.

Her eyes grew large and round as I drew near. Her gaze dropped to my cock, and she licked her lips.

"Oh, and you big, bad beast, don't you dare rip this. It was expensive. And..." She paused for effect as she ran her hands over her abdomen, down toward her pussy. "There is a built-in hole down here for your cock."

I lost control. The beast pounced, lifting her in my arms as I claimed her mouth with my own. Her lush body cushioned mine as I carried her to the wall where I found a ledge nearly identical to the one I'd built in my home. I settled her hips on the ledge. My beast did not ask, simply grabbed her wrists in his hand and lifted them above her head where the magnetized holding links were activated, locking her mating cuffs and her arms over her head.

Satisfied, I took one step back and inspected the bounty before me.

Fuck.

She was lush. Curves everywhere. Soft. Her breasts were full. Her hips wide and curved, her soft thighs open, and her pussy, as she had promised, on display through a designed opening at the base of her costume.

Her pussy glistened, wet and shining, eager for my cock. My fingers. My mouth.

I could not decide which one should taste her first.

My beast, however, had no such hesitation. He knelt between her thighs and locked his mouth around her mound, sucking and tasting, stabbing his tongue deep. The taste of our mate, the sweet tang of her arousal invaded his senses like a drug, and I knew we would both be addicted until the day we died. I would never get enough of her. Her taste. Her smell. The sound coming from her throat as I fucked her with my tongue.

I lifted both hands to play with her nipples, tugging and pulling as I drank down her sweetness, suckled and teased her clit.

She shuddered, held her breath as her body moved closer to release.

My beast stood, denied her release, wanted her orgasm squeezing my cock.

"Maxus!" Her cry of protest drove my beast to hurry. I placed the tip of my cock at her entrance and rubbed her clit with the hard, round head until her breathing was so ragged I feared she might faint. She was out of control, and my beast relished seeing her this way.

"Naughty kitty." I loved everything about this moment. Her black lingerie. The sparkling jewels on top of her collarbone and wrapped around her black gloves. The pointy kitten ears. The way her hazel eyes were locked with mine. The wet, wet pussy so swollen and sensitive and ready for my cock.

"I'll be good, I promise. I'll be good. Let me come. Please."

The *please* rocked me to my core. The pleasure of her surrender sent a blast of fire down my spine and straight to my cock, which jerked in my palm as if it had a life of its own, precum coating my fingertips and her pussy as I teased us both. "Mine."

"Yes. God yes. I thought you were a beast. Hurry up."

My beast was actually chuckling with laughter as he entered her body slowly, bit by bit, relishing the tight heat wrapped around my cock. Pulsing. Throbbing. Squeezing.

"Oh God." Vivian threw her head back and cried out as her release rocketed through her. Her pussy clamped down on my cock, milking and squeezing my hard length, drawing me deeper with each spasm.

I thrust deep, filling her completely as her orgasm shook her entire body, enjoying her pleasure, the dazed look in her eyes.

Her hips rolled, trying to take me deeper, force me to move.

"Maxus."

I knew what she wanted. More. More fucking. More rubbing. She wanted me to push deep over and over until she was crying and moaning and begging me to never stop.

I had heard these things before, but my beast had not. He had never had his cock buried deep, nor felt her wet heat pulse around his length with our mate's pleasure.

The beast moved slowly, pulling back, thrusting forward. Each movement of her body was living art. So beautiful. So fucking perfect.

She was giving us everything, her body, her pleasure, her submission. And still my beast wanted more. Needed more. This was not enough.

With a growl of pain that was more mental than physical, I released her wrists from their restraints in the wall and wrapped my arms around her curved ass, stepped back, carrying her with me as she rode my cock.

Immediately her arms came down around my head, her fingers buried in the beast's hair. She leaned forward, curving her body around mine, trying to get closer, as if it were possible to melt into me. One body. One being.

This was what I needed. Her touch, acceptance, tenderness, love. I could feel her love in her hands, in the way she covered my chest with kisses as she shifted her hips, rubbed her body against mine, rode my cock and took what she wanted.

Me.

Curling my torso around her, I buried my face in her hair, settled my lips against her head, breathed her in as she consumed me. Fucked me. Rode me. Used me. Loved me. *Needed me.*

Her body raced to orgasm, her pleasure in her voice, in the love bites on my chest, the way her hands curled and her fingernails bit into my flesh. "Maxus."

"Vivian." My beast whispered her name as my cock swelled and my seed exploded from my body with the power of a storm so strong I stumbled, turned to brace my back to the wall so I could give her everything. Everything.

When I could breathe, my beast and I at peace, at home in Vivian's body, I was not prepared for the taste of tears running down my own cheeks.

Atlan warlords did not cry.

Atlan beasts didn't even know how. But we cried now, both of us, unable to stop the eruption of emotions that had been locked inside for so many years, through so much killing and struggle and torture. Vivian was a miracle. A fucking miracle that neither of us deserved.

Somehow she knew, even with my cock buried deep and her head pressed to my chest, she knew.

"Maxus?"

"Hmmm?"

"I love you."

The tears came harder. Faster. My cock twitched, all too eager to take her again. The storm rose, and I could not resist her pull. I fucked her. Filled her. Loved her. Gave her my heart, my body, my soul.

My tears.

My breakdown was excruciating. And beautiful. Would have been impossible without her.

"I love you." I would never be able to tell her often enough.

"I love you, too." Her tear streaked cheek was pressed over my heart. She wrapped her arms around my chest and held me. Comforted me. Loved me. "You're mine now. They can't take you away from me? They won't hurt you?"

"I am yours."

She shuddered, her arms tightening. "Good. Because if they ever pull that bullshit again, I am going to kill them myself."

My beast laughed at the idea of her attacking a group of warlords in order to protect me. She was fierce, my mate. My heart.

I was hers, my love, loyalty, and devotion for her and no other.

Now. Tomorrow. Forever.

EPILOGUE

ivian, Planet Atlan, three months later

"THIS PLACE IS HORRIFYING." I walked with my mate, my hand in his as we entered the third corridor of holding cells. We had been here several times before, assisting the doctors with their research, but we had not come through this section of the "medical facility."

I didn't argue with the Atlans, but this place was a prison. Every compartment—containment cell—housed an Atlan warlord on the verge of execution, lost to mating fever, losing control for the last time.

"This is how it has always been." Maxus spoke, but there was resignation in his tone, not disagreement.

"Well, it sucks." Adrian's soft reprimand came from just behind me. She walked next to her sister, both wearing soft, flowing Atlan gowns exactly like mine. I had chosen a warm cinnamon color because Maxus said it reminded him of my hair. Adrian was wearing a soft ivory. Stefani had chosen sunshine yellow. My daughters were here for their first visit to Atlan and had jumped at the chance to slip into the flowing, feminine gowns all the Atlan females wore.

I had to admit, I liked the clothes. I loved my mate. Our home was a freaking *mansion,* the gardens well-tended and stretching as far as I could see from the balcony attached to our bedroom. The home had come complete with staff eager to honor a warlord who had served his people. They were well-paid and had been interviewed and hand selected by Maxus's extended family the moment they'd learned he was still alive.

I'd met cousins, aunts, and uncles. Maxus's parents were no longer living, but the rest of his family had welcomed him back with open arms.

The night he'd been reunited with them all, we'd retired to our rooms and he'd cried until morning. Then he'd fucked me until I couldn't remember my own name, let alone what planet we were on.

My big, bad beast was a big old softy. Total marshmallow. Absolute mush on the inside. But that was our little secret. His and mine. To everyone else he was the unbelievable badass who had survived several years of torture, defeated the psychic attack of Nexus Six, and managed to live, undetected, on Earth long enough to find and claim a mate.

On Atlan, he was a goddamned legend. Legend or not, he was mine. That was all I cared about.

Maxus had explained to me, prior to our transport to Atlan, that warlords who returned from the Hive war were lavished with wealth, land, and gifts as a thank-you from the people of their planet.

It was a far cry from the way veterans were treated back on Earth. The shocking difference almost made me ashamed to be human. Or at least an Earthling. I'd seen some other aliens that looked almost exactly like us. From other planets. Everis. Viken. I was sure there were more.

I'd had a hard time when Dr. Surnen, a Prillon, had appeared at our home to speak to Maxus.

In fact, I'd grabbed a garden tool and swung it at his head, screaming at the top of my lungs that we were under attack.

Luckily the doctor had forgiven me. Maxus had felt so badly about not explaining the fact that the Prillons were, in fact, in charge of the whole damn war, that they were the *good guys,* that he'd spent an entire day in bed with me, making sure I would forgive him.

I'd made him work for it. *Hard.*

Even now, the memories made me flush with heat.

Maxus was so sensitive to my moods that he looked down at me, a speculative—and sexy—gleam in his eye. "Are you well?"

"You know I'm fine." I squeezed his hand. *Hard.* "Behave." I said it out loud, but I was directing the order at myself. It was difficult to obey when I had the sexiest being alive available and eager to get me naked every moment of every day. I'd turned into a nymphomaniac.

He grinned and my heart did a little flip-flop inside my chest. Every time. All he had to do was smile and I fell in love with him all over again.

"If you will come this way, Dr. Surnen has been

working with our medical staff to recreate the effects of the dampening field caused by your specialized integrations," the huge Atlan walking in front of us explained as we followed him down the corridor. "The Hive were definitely on to something. The integrations lining your skull and spinal column appear to have a rather marked effect on suppressing the more aggressive aspects of mating fever. We believe if we can harness this technology, replicate it correctly, we could give many Atlans months, perhaps years of additional time to find a mate."

Maxus seemed unaffected, but I knew he was far from it. He hated the Hive. He hated Nexus Six and everything that monster had done to him. But my mate had a heart bigger than the entire planet. He had allowed them to poke and prod and *drill* into his *skull*. I knew. I sat next to him and held his hand, stayed by his side for every procedure, every test. I was not taking any chances that they were going to try something they shouldn't...like, shoot him dead on the floor of a fight club.

No. I didn't trust any of them with my mate. Probably never would.

Maxus thought my protective instincts were adorable.

I'd show these assholes adorable if they ever tried anything like that again. I'd had a nice long discussion with Warden Egara before I left Earth. I had a few tricks up my sleeve, thanks to her. If any of these guys tried to mess with my man, they were in for a very, very bad time.

I stayed with him during the medical procedures and stripped him naked immediately after to erase the sting of memories no one should have to endure.

He was a god among men—males. Hell, he was just a god. And he was mine.

"All these guys have this fever?" Stefani's voice sounded shocked and mortified. "That's so messed up. What kind of evolutionary advantage would create something that killed males of the species in their prime?"

The Atlan doctor heard her question and stopped. We stood in front of a large elevator that I knew would take us to the medical labs. He looked at Stefani with respect. "This is natural selection, evolution, at its most efficient. If a male is not accepted as mate by his chosen female, his imminent death would eliminate his inferior genetics from the breeding pool. The other males, those worthy, chosen by females to breed and bear children, pass their superior genetics on to the next generation."

Stefani's jaw dropped. "But from what I understand, these guys never even found a female their beast wanted. How is that helpful to the breeding pool? If they don't even have a chance?"

Adrian tilted her head as if thinking about Stefani's question, but I knew she was listening to the odd rumbling and occasional grunts, groans, and roars coming from the beasts who were locked up in the facility. I initially had been captivated—and horrified—by the sounds as well.

The doctor continued as I moved closer to Maxus. I didn't like to think about how close he had been to dying. What my life would have been like if I'd never met him.

"If the beast is not compatible with any of the available females, if his beast does not feel compelled to choose one from among the breeding population, then he is obviously not compatible with the genetic lineages of any fertile females. Therefore his elimination from the breeding pool is still beneficial to the evolution of the species."

"Jeez, you guys are harsh. That sounds terrible to me."

The doctor inclined his head in a slight bow. "I do not mean to upset you. My apologies."

I beamed, so proud that my girls were here, dressing in Atlan clothing, exploring this world with me. They were only staying for a few weeks over their school's scheduled break, but I was thrilled to have them with us.

Maxus wrapped his arm around my waist, his hand coming to rest on my hip, his gaze focused on Adrian as well. He was their de facto father and protector here. I was not surprised to see my pride in our daughters reflected in his eyes. I leaned into his heat. God, I loved him. So much.

"No problem. I just, being an Atlan sounds difficult." Stefani waived it off as Adrian took a step back from the group, craning her head to peek down a corridor off to one side, an area of the facility we had not visited.

The elevator arrived and the doctor stepped to the side, indicating that we should precede him into the space.

Such gentlemen, these Atlans. All of them. Honorable to a fault.

Life here, their culture, their respect for women— females—was such a stark contrast to my life growing up back home that I had to pinch myself once in a while to remind myself that these guys were real. The Atlan females were wonderful as well. Generous and kind. Compassionate. They were huge, every single female I'd seen well over six feet tall, but their gentle natures made them a joy to be around.

We'd only been here a short time, and I already had more friends who genuinely cared about me than I'd ever had on Earth. I had a job I liked, helping out at the local medical facility, learning how to use all the gadgets and gizmos like the ReGen wand Warden Egara had used to heal Maxus's broken fingers after the big fight in Snook's club.

I didn't know what had happened to the two Prillons who attacked me. Didn't want to know or ever think about them again. I didn't know what had been done with Wayne's body. But he'd been friends with Snook for a long time, so I assumed he'd been properly taken care of. And I still didn't know what had happened to my brother. Maxus was making inquiries, but we hadn't heard anything yet. My brother's last known location had been on a battleship way out in space, on the front lines. The Coalition Fleet representative said it might take weeks to track him down due to "the volatile nature of the sector."

I took that as code for *he's probably dead and we just don't want to tell you.*

Unfortunately Maxus agreed. Dead or captured by the Hive, were what my mate considered to be the two most likely options.

And I had sworn I would never go to outer space, never ever become an Interstellar Bride. Never, ever, *ever* marry an alien. With a happy grin, I rubbed my cheek against Maxus's chest, just to remind him that I loved him.

Destiny, it seemed, had a funny sense of humor.

We stood on the elevator platform as Stefani joined us. Then the Atlan doctor.

I froze, my maternal instincts suddenly screaming in alarm. "Where is Adrian?"

Maxus stepped away from me so fast my head spun. He was off the elevator and at the end of the corridor in the space of a heartbeat.

"Stop, Adrian! Do not!" He shouted the command, and my heart dropped into the pit of my stomach. Shit. Shit. Shit. What was wrong? What was happening to my daughter?

I ran for Maxus, saw Adrian beyond him, halfway down the next corridor. I rushed for her, but Maxus grabbed me around the waist and swung me off my feet to prevent me from moving any closer.

Stefani came up behind us, the doctor placing himself between her and whatever was happening farther down the corridor.

There, Adrian stood, hand raised to the control panel belonging to one of the containment cells.

"Baby girl? What are you doing? Get away from there," I yelled.

She turned to face me, and the ashen shock on her face made me shake. "I can't."

"Adrian? What's up?" Stefani called to her twin. "Talk to me."

Adrian responded to her twin, as I had hoped she would. She turned her body to face us, her hand blessedly removed from the control panel I knew would unleash a raging, violent beast. "I can't leave him here."

"Who?" Stefani asked. "Can't leave who?"

Adrian shrugged, then turned to look at the beast locked in the cell. "I don't know. I don't know who he is."

"Then what are you doing?" I asked.

My daughter walked to the cell and leaned forward, resting her forehead against the energy field that separated her from the beast inside. She lifted her hand and pressed her palm flat, as a toddler would to a glass window. "They can't kill him, Mom."

"Daughter, he's here because he has mating fever." Maxus spoke slowly, clearly, his deep voice meant to soothe and calm. "He is dangerous. Out of control. He's probably not even aware of where he is or what he is doing. Do not release him from that cell. He could kill you, try to kill all of us."

"No. No, he won't." Adrian shook her head slowly, rolling her forehead against the energy field, looking at the beast within. "He's mine."

A SPECIAL THANK YOU TO MY READERS...

Want more? I've got *hidden* bonus content on my web site *exclusively* for those on my mailing list.

If you are already on my email list, you don't need to do a thing! Simply scroll to the bottom of my newsletter emails and click on the *super-secret* link.

Not a member? What are you waiting for? In addition to ALL of my bonus content (great new stuff will be added regularly) you will be the first to hear about my newest release the second it hits the stores—AND you will get a free book as a special welcome gift.

Sign up now! http://freescifiromance.com

FIND YOUR INTERSTELLAR MATCH!

YOUR mate is out there. Take the test today and discover your perfect match. Are you ready for a sexy alien mate (or two)?

VOLUNTEER NOW!

interstellarbridesprogram.com

DO YOU LOVE AUDIOBOOKS?

Grace Goodwin's books are now available as
audiobooks...everywhere.

LET'S TALK!

Interested in joining my **Sci-Fi Squad**? Meet new like-minded sci-fi romance fanatics and chat with Grace! Get excerpts, cover reveals and sneak peeks before anyone else. Be part of a private Facebook group that shares pictures and fun news! Join here:

https://www.facebook.com/groups/scifisquad/

Want to talk about Grace Goodwin books with others? Join the **SPOILER ROOM** and spoil away! Your GG BFFs are waiting! (And so is Grace) Join here:

https://www.facebook.com/groups/ggspoilerroom/

GET A FREE BOOK!

JOIN MY MAILING LIST TO BE THE FIRST TO KNOW OF NEW RELEASES, FREE BOOKS, SPECIAL PRICES AND OTHER AUTHOR GIVEAWAYS.

http://freescifiromance.com

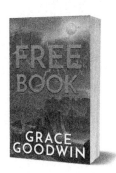

ALSO BY GRACE GOODWIN

Surprise Mates

Interstellar Brides® Program Boxed Set - Books 6-8

Interstellar Brides® Program Boxed Set - Books 9-12

Interstellar Brides® Program Boxed Set - Books 13-16

Interstellar Brides® Program Boxed Set - Books 17-20

Interstellar Brides® Program: The Colony

Surrender to the Cyborgs

Mated to the Cyborgs

Cyborg Seduction

Her Cyborg Beast

Cyborg Fever

Rogue Cyborg

Cyborg's Secret Baby

Her Cyborg Warriors

Claimed by the Cyborgs

The Colony Boxed Set 1

The Colony Boxed Set 2

The Colony Boxed Set 3

Interstellar Brides® Program: The Virgins

The Alien's Mate

His Virgin Mate

Claiming His Virgin

His Virgin Bride

His Virgin Princess

The Virgins - Complete Boxed Set

Interstellar Brides® Program: Ascension Saga

Ascension Saga, book 1

Ascension Saga, book 2

Ascension Saga, book 3

Trinity: Ascension Saga - Volume 1

Ascension Saga, book 4

Ascension Saga, book 5

Ascension Saga, book 6

Faith: Ascension Saga - Volume 2

Ascension Saga, book 7

Ascension Saga, book 8

Ascension Saga, book 9

Destiny: Ascension Saga - Volume 3

Interstellar Brides® Program: The Beasts

Bachelor Beast

Maid for the Beast

Beauty and the Beast

The Beasts Boxed Set

Starfighter Training Academy

The First Starfighter

Starfighter Command

Elite Starfighter

Starfighter Training Academy Boxed Set

Other Books

Dragon Chains

Their Conquered Bride

Wild Wolf Claiming: A Howl's Romance

ABOUT GRACE

Grace Goodwin is a USA Today and international bestselling author of Sci-Fi and Paranormal romance with over a million books sold. Grace's titles are available worldwide on all retailers, in multiple languages, and in ebook, print, audio and other reading App formats.

Grace is a full-time writer whose earliest movie memories are of Luke Skywalker, Han Solo, and real, working light sabers. (Still waiting for Santa to come through on that one.) Now Grace writes sexy-as-hell sci-fi romance six days a week. In her spare time, she reads, watches campy sci-fi and enjoys spending time with family and friends. No matter where she is, there is always a part of her dreaming up new worlds and exciting characters for her next book.

Grace loves to chat with readers and can frequently be found lurking in her Facebook groups. Interested in joining her **Sci-Fi Squad**? Meet new like-minded sci-fi romance fanatics and chat with Grace! Get excerpts, cover reveals and sneak peeks before anyone else. Join here: https://www.facebook.com/groups/scifisquad/

Want to talk about Grace Goodwin books with others? Join the **SPOILER ROOM** and spoil away! Your GG BFFs are waiting! (And so is Grace) Join here:

https://www.facebook.com/groups/ggspoilerroom/

Printed in Great Britain
by Amazon